P9-CJU-869
3 1404 00754 3462

Beatle Dreams
and other stories

Beatle Dreams
and other stories

by
Guillermo Samperio

translated by
Russell M. Cluff &
L. Howard Quackenbush

Latin American Literary Review Press
Series: Discoveries
Pittsburgh, Pennsylvania
1994

The Latin American Literary Review Press publishes Latin American creative writing under the series title *Discoveries*, and critical works under the series title *Explorations*.

Library of Congress Cataloging-in-Publication Data

Samperio, Guillermo.
[Selections. 1990. English]
Beatle dreams and other stories / by Guillermo Samperio ; translated by Russell M. Cluff and L. Howard Quackenbush.
p. cm. -- (Discoveries)
Originally published: Antología personal, 1971-1990. Xalapa, México : Universidad Veracruzana, 1990.
ISBN 0-935480-60-9 : $15.95
I. Title. II. Series.
PQ7298.A414A5813 1993
863--dc20 92-21225
CIP

Cover design by Lisa Pallo. Book design by Susan Wackerbarth.

The paper used in this publication meets the minimum requirements of the American National Standard for Permanence for Printed Library Materials Z39.48.1984. ♾

Beatle Dreams and Other Stories may be ordered directly from the publisher:

Latin American Literary Review Press
121 Edgewood Avenue
Pittsburgh, PA 15218
Tel (412) 371-9023 • Fax (412) 371-9025

Acknowledgments

This project is supported in part by grants from the National Endowment for the Arts in Washington, D.C., a federal agency; the Commonwealth of Pennsylvania Council on the Arts, Brigham Young University, and Fundación Cultural Bancomer, Mexico. Fundación Cultural Bancomer

The stories in this collection were first published in Spanish as follows:

"Cuando el tacto toma la palabra," and "Datos biológicos" in *Cuando el tacto toma la palabra* (1974); "Después de la puerta," "Se vale de todo," "Yurécuaro," and "Fuera del ring" in *Fuera del ring* (1975); "Tomando vuelo" in *Tomando vuelo y demás cuentos* (1976); "Lenin en el fútbol," "En el departamentito del tiempo," "Aquí Georgina," and "Una noche de noticias" in *Lenin en el fútbol* (1978); "Tiempo libre," "La señorita Green," "Las sombras," and "Dr. Mane" in *Textos extraños* (1981); "El Hombre de la penumbra," "El Hombre de las llaves," "La Gertrudis," "Mañanita blusera," "Sencilla mujer de mediodía," "Complicada mujer de tarde," "Relato con jacaranda," "Sueños de escarabajo," "Bodas de fuego," and "Ella habitaba un cuento" in *Gente de la ciudad* (1986); "La cochinilla," "Algunas muertes," "Estación fatal," "Místicas serpientes," "Lombrices," "Zapatos de tacón rojos para mujer linda," "Carta del pirata Witold," "Zapatos de tacón negros para la mujer linda de los zapatos de tacón rojos," "Zapatos de tacón amarillos," "Te amo," "Zapatos de tacón blancos," "Zapatos de tacón grises," and "Del zapatero" in *Cuaderno imaginario* (1990).

Contents

introduction

Guillermo Samperio was born in Mexico City, October 22, 1948. He is considered one of Mexico's finest contemporary short story writers with a total production of over 170 stories, appearing in more than ten volumes; he has written one novel (entitled *Ventriloquia inalámbrica* [Wireless Ventriloquy]) and is working on a second. He has served as a coordinator of numerous literary workshops, is an art critic, an editor, and is currently the vice-president of the Asociación de Escritores Mexicanos [Association of Mexican Writers]. Samperio has served as assistant director and, then, director of the Literature Section of the National Institute of Fine Arts between 1986 and 1990.

Gente de la ciudad [The City's People] (1986) is one of his most accomplished collections comprising multifaceted vignettes that coalesce into a mosaic of Mexico City. It extends far beyond geographical limits to encompass the "spiritual" essence of the metropolis. His last three books are *Cuaderno imaginario* [Imaginary Journal] (1990), *Antología personal* [Personal Anthology], and *El hombre de la penumbra* [The Keeper of the Shadows] (1991). The first of these, *Cuaderno imaginario*, represents his most in-depth development of diverse micro-genres: the epigram, the maxim, the fable, the micro-story, the prose poem, the palindrome. The last two, *Antología personal* and *El hombre de la penumbra,* constitute a compilation of the author's favorite tales.

Samperio is known as a master of various literary postures: the self-referential or metafictional story, the micro-story, poetic portraiture, stories of irony and subtly veiled humor, and well-rounded tales of significant social content. He is intrigued by the idiosyncrasies of the human condition, which makes him an extraordinary observer of human nature. He never strays far from those themes critical to life itself, for example, male-female views of sexuality, music and its impact upon the human psyche, or the megalopolis as seen through the eyes of the common man, laborers and bureaucrats. He is especially fond of the anthropomorphic conceptualization of the story as a living entity—oftentimes portraying the natural forces that face the writer as a human being (for example, the character Textófaga—devourerer of texts—in the story "Dr. Mane"). Another mode developed (perhaps even created) by Samperio is the brief allegory in which an inanimate entity assumes human characteristics and symbolizes certain aspects of life (as in "Fire Wedding"). Samperio continuously toys with the prejudices and the fashionable fetishes of his contemporaries, as exemplified in the "poetic portraits" of women, such as "Midday's Unpretentious Woman" and "Complicated Woman of the Afternoon" (based on real-life subjects). A significant, yet easily overlooked, aspect of Samperio's craftsmanship lies in his use of tone. Much of his seemingly serious prose is actually tongue-in-cheek humor. "Yurécuaro," for example, is an initiation story that goes far beyond the traditional mode, combining the poetic, the erotic, the rural and the urban, laced with a youthful, picaresque humor.

He has won numerous national and international literary prizes: El Museo del Chopo prize (1976, for the story "Bodegón" [Warehouse]), "La Palabra y el Hombre" (1977, given by the Universidad Veracruzana for "Desnuda" [A Nude]), the "Casa de las Américas" prize (Havana, Cuba, 1977, for his book *Lenin en el fútbol* [Lenin and Soccer]), and the Belisario Domínguez prize (1988, for *Cuaderno imaginario* [Imaginary Journal]).

Samperio's bibliography is composed of the following works: *Cuando el tacto toma la palabra* [When Touch Becomes Word], México: Ediciones de Difusión Cultural del IPN, 1974; *Fuera del ring* [Outside the Ring], México: INBA, 1975; *Cruz y cuernos* [The Cross and the Horns of the Beast] México: Ed. El Mendrugo, 1976; *Tomando vuelo y demás cuentos* [Wind-up and Other Stories], Xalapa, Veracruz: Universidad Veracruzana, 1976; *Lenin en el fútbol* [Lenin and Soccer], México: Grijalbo, 1978; *Manifiesto de amor* [Manifesto of Love], México: Ediciones El Tucán de Virginia, 1980; *Textos extraños* [Strange Tales], México: Folios Ediciones, 1981; *De este lado y del otro* (poems) [On This Side and on the Other], Ediciones Papel de Envolver (Colección Luna Hiena), Xalapa: Universidad Veracruzana, 1982; *Miedo ambiente y otros miedos* [Ambience of Fear and Other Phobias], México: Secretaría de Educación Pública, 1986; *Gente de la ciudad* [The City's People], México: Fondo de Cultura Económica, 1986; *El hombre equivocado* (novel, co-author) [The Mistaken Man], México: Joaquín Mortiz, 1989; *Cuaderno imaginario* [Imaginary Journal], México: Diana, 1990; *Antología personal (1971-1990): Ellos habitaban un cuento* [Personal Anthology (1971-1990): They Lived in a Story], Xalapa, Veracruz: Universidad Veracruzana, 1990; *El hombre de la penumbra* [The Keeper of the Shadows], Caracas, Venezuela: Alfadil Ediciones, 1991.

The editors/translators wish to acknowledge their appreciation for the generous contributions made toward this publication by the David M. Kennedy Center for International Studies and the College of Humanities of Brigham Young University.

R.M.C.
L.H.Q.

she lived in a story

for Fernando Ferreira de Loanda

When we believe we are dreaming and we are awake, we experience *vertigo of the mind.*

Silvina Ocampo and Adolfo Bioy Casares

During the evening hours, the writer Guillermo Segovia gave a talk at the Preparatory Academy of Iztapalapa. The aesthetics students, under the direction of the young poet Israel Castellanos, were enthusiastic about Segovia's detailed presentation. Professor Castellanos did not neglect to thank and praise the lecturer's work in front of the students. The one who was most pleased was Segovia himself, for even though, before beginning, he felt a little nervous, once he began explaining the notes he had prepared two days earlier, his words flowed with strength and ease. When a young man asked about the creation of characters inspired by real people, Guillermo Segovia was secretly disappointed that the emotion and confidence that had overcome him had not been displayed before a more sophisticated audience. Such a vain idea had not deterred him from enjoying a certain giddiness because of his creative and sharply defined words, that space in which his theory and examples converge in a solid and, at the same time, simple discourse. He allowed phrases to intertwine without being too conscious of them, and the interaction of words produced an obvious dynamic, independent of voice.

Guillermo Segovia had just turned thirty-four; he had three books of stories, a novel and a series of newspaper articles published both domestically and abroad, particularly in France, where he received his degree in literature. When he returned to Mexico, six years before his speech at the Academy, he married Elena, a young Colombian researcher, and they had two children. At the time of his return, the writer took a job working at a newspaper, while his wife worked at the National University of Mexico. They rented a small house in old Coyoacán where they lived comfortably.

Now on his way home, driving an '82 VW, Guillermo could not remember several passages from the end of his presentation. But it didn't bother him too much; his memory was prone to sporadic lapses. Besides, he was excited about one part that he did remember, and which he could use to write a story. It had to do with that witty comparison he had made between an architect and a writer. "From the creative point of view the design of a home is invariably found within the realm of the fictitious; by the time the bricklayers begin to build it, we are already witnessing the fulfillment of that fiction. Once the house is finished, the owner will inhabit the house and the fiction of the architect. Extending this line of reasoning, we might say that cities are fictions of architecture; for that reason the latter is considered an art form. The architect who lives in a house that he designed and built himself is one of the few persons who can possibly live in his own fantasy. From his perspective the author is an architect of words, who designs stories and sentences so that the reader may live in the text. A house and a story should be solid, functional, necessary, lasting. In a story, one might say, movement demands fluidity, from the living room to the kitchen, or from the bedrooms to the bath. No unnecessary columns or walls. The different sections of the story or of the house should be indispensable and created with precision. Literature is written and homes are built so that man may live in them in comfort."

"Live in a text," Guillermo couldn't stop thinking as his car traveled through the night down Iztapalapa Avenue. The only thing he paid attention to were the stoplights, and nothing of the sordid panorama of that part of the city caught his eye. Not even when the traffic became heavier around Calzada de la Viga did he notice the change in direction. "Live in a text," he kept insisting, despite his mental blanks. The idea of inhabiting words overwhelmed him. Suddenly he wanted to create a story around that idea. Imagining how to accomplish it, he thought he'd attempt to eliminate literary solutions for similar themes. Out of the blue he said to himself that a woman would be the appropriate character. Through a haze, he visualized a woman living in a story created by him. "She lived in the text" was the first transformation. "Now I'm already in the domain of the story; the sentence itself is literary, it sounds good."

He remembered several women, near and distant, but none of them met his requirements. He went back and began by imagining her activities. He created a small catalogue of professions and tasks, finally leaning toward actresses. He wondered about the reasons for his selection, as his car sped away from the Country Club neighborhood and headed toward Miguel Angel de Quevedo, in order to cross the Tlalpan bridge. He gave full rein to his thoughts in search of an answer or a justification. "In one way or another actors live in the text. They live the part they were given to play and they also live the text; they do not embody anyone at all. In the theater they live in literature for a brief moment. In motion pictures, some of their moments endure tending toward the eternal. Dramatists have written plays in an attempt to approach the ancient dream of the fiction writer: that human beings live in their texts. That artistic creation transcends the imaginary level so as to become real. With regard to my own concept, the movement is reversed, that is, reality moves toward the imaginary."

Guillermo Segovia's car turned onto Felipe Carrillo Puerto, advanced a block and turned toward Alberto Zamora. Thirty meters ahead it came to a stop. As he turned off the engine he decided that the woman in this story would be a young actress whom he admired for her performances and her extraordinary beauty. Furthermore, the actress somewhat resembled the painter Frida Kahlo, who painted herself in the dreams of her paintings, another way to live in one's own fiction. Although Segovia did not give a title to his works before writing them, on this occasion he had an urge to do so. "She Lived in a Story" would be the title of his tale. The woman's name, just like the actual actress', would be Ofelia.

Guillermo got out of the VW and went into his house. Passing through a modest living room on his left, he entered the study, a small room whose walls were covered floor to ceiling with book shelves. He turned on the light, took the typewriter out of its case, put it on the desk at the other end of the room, next to the window, through which a few plants in the small garden could be seen. He turned on the radio of his sound system and tuned in *Radio Universidad*. When he opened the top desk drawer, Elena appeared in the doorway.

"How did it go?" she said walking toward him.

"Fine," Guillermo answered moving in her direction.

They kissed; Segovia caressed her hair and hips. They kissed again, and separating, Elena repeated:

"How did the people react?"

"They were quite interested. I realized that the boys had read my stories, which of course I owe to Castellanos . . . During the discussion an interesting idea came up," he started to explain, walking over to the desk.

"The children just went to bed . . . I was reading a little . . . don't you want something to eat?"

"No . . . I'd rather start writing . . ."

"Okay. I'll wait for you in the bedroom."

Elena left the room blowing a kiss toward her husband off the palms of her hands. Guillermo Segovia settled down in front of his typewriter. Then from the drawer that he had left open, he took out several sheets of blank paper and inserted the first one. He typed the title and began to write.

She Lived in a Story

That day the cold wave intensified in the city. Sometime around eleven o'clock that night, a fog settled in, brought on by the low temperature and the smog. The darkness was denser than usual and it gave an eerie feeling to even the brightest areas. The old streets in the center of Coyoacán were reminiscent of scenes from centuries past. Even the light coming from street lights and cars seemed shadowy, only slightly penetrating that ancient space. Only a few people dressed in top coats or heavy sweaters and scarves were out walking, hugging the walls, trying to ward off the cold. They looked like silhouettes from another time, as if from this Coyoacán had emerged a Coyoacán from the past and the people had mistaken the century, heading for places they would never find. Ofelia walked away from Plaza Hidalgo, heading down the narrow Francisco Sosa Avenue. Her slender figure was clad in gray woolen slacks and a heavy black sweater which because of its bagginess seemed to hang from her shoulders. A violet scarf encircled the woman's long neck. The white skin of her face was a tenuous light that stood out against the dark hair, which brushed her shoulders as she moved. The sound of her black boots on the flagstones was barely audible.

Ofelia sensed she was being watched, although it was impossible to ascertain from which direction. At the corner of Francisco Sosa and Ave María she stopped as a car turned to the right. She took advantage of this instant to look behind her, presuming she would see the person who was watching her. She saw only an old couple who stepped out of a doorway and headed for the Plaza. Before crossing the street she felt vulnerable. Then, she experienced a slight shudder. She thought that perhaps it would have been better if someone had been following her. She started walking again confident that, although she was alone, the night was watching her movements. She became frightened and instinctively began to walk faster. She rubbed her hands, looked toward the trees in front of her and then all the way down the avenue that receded into the foggy mist. "It would have been better if I had let them give me a ride," she lamented as she was about to cross Ayuntamiento Street.

Minutes earlier, she had been in the old structure of the Center for Dramatic Arts watching the dress rehearsal of a play from the Middle Ages. When the rehearsal was over and after they went out into the street, one of the actresses offered to give her a ride. Ofelia came up with the excuse that she had to visit a friend who lived right around the corner, on Francisco Sosa. The truth was that the eerie, gray atmosphere of Coyoacán had given her the urge to walk. Furthermore, for her, the foggy atmosphere was a continuation of the staging of the play and it reminded her of the time she spent in England. She said good-bye and started walking, while all the others got into their cars.

First she had felt the impression of being watched while walking down the avenue. Now she found no real reason to be afraid, realizing that nothing special was happening to her. This phenomenon should have had a rational explanation, but for the moment she couldn't figure it out. She found this idea comforting and, more encouraged, she warmed her hands by blowing on them. Nevertheless this sudden ease of mind heightened her perceptive abilities. No doubt, there were eyes attempting to look inside her; eyes whose function seemed to be of a tactile nature.

Fine, it was impossible for her to separate herself from life's experience, but she still wanted to understand. Were these feelings new and therefore without any possible explanation? What were those inquisitive eyes searching for? Seldom had she experienced feelings of persecution: she accepted a certain amount of insecurity, given the violence of Mexico City. She moved with caution. Now that she really was exposing herself, no one was threatening her. The people in the few cars passing by paid no attention to her. Then she remembered the brightly lit spaces on the stage, when the glare of the spotlights did not permit her to see the audience, who in turn was looking at her. She knows that a multitude of eyes are out there in the dark, moving to the rhythm she establishes: many eyes, one large concealed eye, one giant eye fixed on her body. Seeking to bolster herself with this recollection, Ofelia told herself that perhaps it had to do with her skin's own memory, foreign to her mind; in that murky landscape perhaps it had returned to her body and was gradually possessing it. Eye-network, eye-space, large eye coming toward her, growing eye; Ofelia tried to escape the sensation by shaking her head. But she knew all along that the effort was useless; exhausted, she abandoned herself to her fate and felt herself sinking into the depths of night. All of a sudden she found herself walking in total darkness, losing her sense of place, yet still with a vague certainty that she was facing no danger.

When she turned into the alley where her house was, she could feel the enormous eye upon her hair, her face, her scarf, her sweater, her slacks. She stopped and felt a kind of dizziness similar to what you experience in a dream in which you float unsupported and without any way of coming down. Ofelia knew that she was only a few meters from her house, in Coyoacán, in her city, on Earth, but at the same time she could not avoid the sensation that it was a dream, and while she experienced vertigo, it was a pleasant feeling because a dreamer in the end knows there is no danger and throws his body into the darkness like a Zeppelin that descends when it is watched. Ofelia remained standing in the alley, trying to understand; in a hushed voice she said to herself: "This is not a fainting spell or a psychological problem. This does not come from me, it's something outside of me, beyond my control." She moved slowly toward the wall and leaned her back against it. The sensation became stronger throughout her slender body, as though the fog in the alley had settled upon her. "It's not that they are still watching me; it's something more powerful." She raised her hand to her forehead and kept running her fingers through her hair. Alarmed, suddenly comprehending the situation, she said to herself: "I'm inside the eye." She lowered her arm slowly and, pursuing the idea expressed in her last words, she continued: "I'm inside the gaze. I live within a stare. I'm part of a manner of seeing. Something compels me to walk; the fog has descended and its murky fingers reach out toward the windows. I'm a silhouette from the past clinging to the walls. My name is Ofelia and I'm opening the wooden gate to my house. I enter. To my right shadow-theater figures appear in the garden, and from among the plants out jumps Paloma eagerly greeting me. Her white coat is like an oval ball of cotton suspended in the darkness. She barks at me timidly, comes up to my legs and rubs against my calves; then she stands on her two hind legs inviting me to play. I pet her and gently push her aside. She growls mournfully, but I am already walking among the plants along the path made with stones from the river bed. The entryway light is on, I open the door, and close it. I want something to eat and I head for the kitchen. I stop and I feel obliged to retrace my steps. I continue on toward the living room. I turn on the floor lamp, I open the bar, I take out a glass and a bottle of cognac. Without closing the bar door, I serve myself and, after taking the first drink, I realize that I still want something to eat, but the taste of the cognac captivates me and, against my will, I decide not to eat. When I lift the glass to my lips the second time, Plácida appears. She greets me respectfully and asks me if she might get me something. I tell her to go to bed, explaining that tomorrow we have to get up early. With a slight bow of the head, Plácida leaves, and I finish my drink. I am carrying the bottle and the glass between my fingers; with my free hand I turn off the lamp and, in the dark, I cross the living room and climb the stairs. The door to my bedroom is open. I enter. I turn on the light. I approach my dressing table. I place the bottle and glass on it. I sit on the seat, open the drawer, take out my notebook, a fountain pen, and I begin to write down what is happening to me."

I know very well that I still live inside the gaze. I hear the sounds that are generated deep within it, similar to the city noises that rise to the top of the Latin American Tower. I have had to move with precision and calm. My fear is disappearing. I'm surprised, with no hint of desperation. All of a sudden, I'm upset, angry. I must write a protest. Yes, a protest, gentlemen. I protest! Men of the world, I protest. I write that I am an inhabitant, I write that my illness has left me. I stop writing. I poured myself a shot of liquor and downed it in one gulp. I really like my old *Montblanc* pen, it has a good point. My body's burning up, my cheeks are red. I'm certain I cannot stop living in two worlds. Francisco Sosa Avenue, which seems so far away from me now, is two roads. One single large eye. Within the streets of this old Coyoacán that I love so much, exists another Coyoacán. I had been walking through two Coyoacáns, through two nights, through the thick fog. At this moment of dizzying revelations, there are people like me, who live in both Coyoacáns; Coyoacáns which coincide perfectly one with the other, neither under nor above each other, just one center and two worlds. Someone, perhaps a man, at this very moment writes down these exact same words that are appearing in my notebook. These very same words. I stop writing. I have another drink. I feel a little tipsy; I'm happy. It is as though my bedroom were flooded with light. Paloma barks at two invisible moons. It occurs to me that I should write that the man's name is most likely Guillermo, he has a beard, and a long straight nose. It could be Guillermo Segovia, the writer, who at the same time lives as another Guillermo Segovia. Guillermo Segovia in Guillermo Samperio, each inside the other, a single body. I insist on thinking that he writes with his typewriter precisely what I write, word after word, one discourse and two worlds. Guillermo writes a story that is too pretentious. The central character could have my name. I write that he writes a story in which I live. It's already after midnight and the writer Guillermo Segovia is tired. He stops writing, he scratches his beard, he twists his mustache; he stands up, he stretches his arms and, while lowering them, he leaves the study. He goes up to the bedrooms on the second floor. He enters his bedroom and sees that his wife is asleep, with an open book on her lap. He goes up to her, kisses her on the cheek, takes the book from her and puts it on the dresser. Before leaving he glances once more at his wife. As he goes downstairs he senses that he is being watched, although he cannot determine from where. He stops and turns, thinking that his youngest son has gotten up, but no one is there. "This is probably a suggestion that comes to me from my own story," he thinks while still trying to figure it out. He goes on down and the sensation grows more intense. This change bothers him because he understands that the next step is knowing that he is not being watched, but rather is living inside a gaze, that he is now part of a new way of seeing. Standing at the foot of the stairs, he thinks: "That gaze could be Ofelia's." To my way of thinking, in what I write with my beautiful *Montblanc,* I feel like I'm moving out of Guillermo Segovia's story. And he cannot pretend that my text might be entitled something like "Guillermo Lived in a Story;" now I write down that Segovia, already scared out of his wits, moves toward his study at the same time that I begin to live in one Coyoacán, while he gradually inhabits two, three, many Coyoacáns. Guillermo picks up the fifteen pages he has written, a half-written story, full of errors; he picks up his lighter, ignites it and touches the flame to the corner of the pages and they begin to burn. He observes how the flames rise from his tale prematurely entitled "She Lived in a Story." He throws the half-burned manuscript into the wastepaper basket, believing that when it stops burning the "suggestion" will cease. But, now, he hears the sounds that are generated deep within my steady gaze, like the city noises that rise to the top of the Latin American Tower. He sees the smoke rise from the wastepaper basket but his fear does not diminish. He wants to go to his wife so she can comfort him, but he senses that it would do no good. Standing in the middle of the study, Guillermo does not know what to do. He knows that he lives in his house and other houses, even though it does not fully register. He walks to his desk, he sits down in front of his typewriter, he opens the second drawer. Overcome by the urgency to halt his disintegration, without knowing exactly what or whom to kill, he takes out the old 38 Colt that he inherited from his grandfather. He stands up, walks toward the door; he carries the weapon pointing up. While he crosses the living room in the darkness, he feels as though he is about to lose consciousness, still holding fast to the idea of the moment he is living. Finally, in that state of confusion and anguish, he returns to the second floor. The room at the back is still lit; he heads in that direction.

Stopping in the doorway, he cannot recognize the bedroom, his eyes are unable to tell him what they are seeing even if they do see. Through his index finger the cold reality of metal begins to flow; he feels the trigger and the grip. A dim light appears in the depths of his perception, helping him recognize the elements of his situation. He distinguishes shapes, shadows of some reality; he looks at his extended arm and raises his eyes. In front of him, seated on a pretty stool, a woman watches him. Segovia slowly lowers his arm and lets the Colt drop, which produces a muffled sound as it hits the rug. The woman stands and tries to force a smile upon her thin lips. When Guillermo realizes that he is not facing any danger, his fear subsides, leaving his body slightly numb. Without thinking he decides to move closer. With the movement of his legs he finally achieves clarity. He stops next to me, in silence, accepting our fate, he takes my hand and I am willing.

beatle dreams

for Maricruz, Eduardo, and Oriana

Alfredo was not exactly what you would call middle-middle class, since, unfortunately, he was a product of the lower middle class. However, like all the kids, he really grooves on *The Beatles*. He has never understood them, well, he has never understood what they say in their songs, but, be that as it may, he still grooves on them. Alfredo must be about thirty years old now; at the time of those evening encounters he was fifteen or sixteen. He wore his uncles' outdated hand-me-downs, those uncles who loved popular Tex-Mex border music and boleros. You could safely say that Alfredo hated his uncles for both reasons: because of the clothes they wore and their musical tastes. He couldn't stand family get-togethers where, half-drunk, out came the guitars and they started in with "Your Lover Has Just Arrived" and ended, now drunk out of their minds, with "Blank Page." No, he just couldn't stand them; he thought that they were all complete idiots, dressed like idiots. But who was responsible for this apparently anti-Mexican attitude? Because there is not a more anti-Mexican attitude than to hate border songs and boleros. It was because of a rock group that many began to call the *Scarabs*, or, in other words, *The Beatles*. If at that moment someone had asked Freddy why blame the English group for his putting on airs, he wouldn't have been able to answer. He simply would have made an ugly face or an obscene gesture with his hand. Regardless, it would have been a real and a profound answer, because two or three years after the commotion caused by *The Beatles*, he wanted to leave home for a few months right in the middle of a big scandal. And he left forever.

The Beatles made him sad, made his pulse quicken, and they made him happy. His imagination took off, and all of a sudden he dreamed that Adela, a beautiful girl who lived a couple of blocks from his house, would throw him a note from the school bus that said, "Let's get together this afternoon in China Park, in the shade of the ahuehuete trees. We can hold hands and no one will bother us. The ahuehuetes will be the stairway that will carry us up to the shoulders of the spacious light blue sky that we dream about every night. And, once on top, we'll kiss."

Then Alfredo found himself approaching the ugly wardrobe that he shared with his little brother and began to choose one of twenty or thirty shirts—all in pastel colors with white collars—until, a little bored, he took out one that was light pink. While putting it on a melody sprang from one of the drawers of that awful wardrobe: *Things We Said Today*; the notes of the melody came out and swirled around his face, became entangled in his hair and then because it was getting late—Adela might arrive there and feel stood up; I'm sure she would begin kicking the ahuehuete trees. Hurriedly, he stuck his arm in his shirt, he took down a gray coat, without lapels or collar, with a hundred buttons that went all the way up to his throat, and threw it on. Without even thinking about the pants and shoes he put on, in a flash, he found himself walking along the path in China Park. There came Adela, still dressed in her school uniform, but with high-heeled shoes over cinnamon-colored school socks. Without saying a word they smiled at one another, they took each other's hand and—as if it were enough just to be young and together—they walked to the foot of the ladder/ahuehuete and ascended, their hands gripping tighter and tighter, and, now on top, on the shoulders of the spacious light blue sky, the musical notes that had sprung from his drawer were now reactivated and burst from Freddy's hair, creating a musical bond between Adela and him. She admired him, she looked at him from the eternal depths of her chestnut eyes—words were still useless—Adela and Alfredo's lips met, the music increased in volume and the world soon began to disappear. The only important things were she and he in the imagination of an Alfredo who was now lying on the top bunk, without his shoes, with one toe sticking out of his sock, wiggling, keeping time, his hands behind his head, all of a sudden hearing his mother shout, "Let's eat," bringing him out of his Beatle dream. With the same vigor that he used to imagine those amorous encounters, he began to hate the elbow macaroni soup and the rice and the stewed meat cooked by the female progenitor who, because of some biological accident, had brought him into this bleary-eyed world. Alfredo could not stop his mounting phobia, and he went on hating: the grown man's belt that almost went around him twice, the grimy walls of his room, the decrepit apartment building where they lived, the streets full of potholes, the San Alvaro district with its doorless, gaudy church, the city that he barely knew, and this country that who knows where it would wind up with its border songs and boleros. Then he would sit down at the table without washing his hands and start digging into one of his ears with his little finger. That evening he was consoled by telling himself that a couple of hours later he would have one of those evening encounters.

When was it that he was shook up by *The Beatles*? Why, without even understanding them totally—a friend had translated a couple of songs for him—did he feel like *The Beatles* were gasoline that drove him to live more fully in his little world, and when did they tell him that things were not going as well as everyone was saying? No, not even now, a married man for seven years and with two kids, could he answer that question to his satisfaction. The best he could do was venture a not-too-certain guess, inspired by two different feelings.

It's true, Alfredo thinks, *The Beatles* have a light side, basically one of love, youthfully melancholic—so much so that nowadays lots of housewives listen to them and, while they complain about this "little hell" they dust off their female Beatle dreams; no one should be surprised: these were the young girls of fifteen years ago. Nevertheless, aside from love, *The Beatles* introduced controversy, sarcasm, play; they opened doors, they pointed at us with their fingers. So, Freddy and everybody else began that uninhibited love affair and shed their thin shells. It was a dormant feeling and the need to throw open the doors was now on the horizon—not too long ago society had to put up with chain-carrying punks, perhaps they themselves, even though with chains swinging, they were now knocking on the door of the "here and the now"—and *The Beatles* arrived right on time, to provide the perfect accompaniment. From this new possibility it was very easy to jump forward to Bob Dylan, Joan Baez, and *The Stones*. Our parents would never have imagined that their children would use electricity to make themselves heard within twenty square blocks.

Freddy went to one of those jam sessions on the evening of the elbow macaroni soup. He put on the best clothes he could find, he polished his shoes; he combed his hair and, in a flash—because he only had to walk two blocks—he found himself leaning up against one of the patio walls at the Sepúlveda's home. On his left and on his right, other kids were chain-smoking their *Fiestas*; a few couples were dancing to Ray Coniff. Lots of girls, their eyes bright with expectation, all sitting in a row, all along the wall across from them, anxiously waiting, talking about everything and about nothing.

Suddenly, a small group sabotaged the record player and, in the middle of the fourth boring Ray Coniff song, the few that were dancing had to stop, both upset and surprised, because the speakers were silent, and the seated girls and the leaning boys began to smile and, then, *She loves you, yeah, yeah, yeah* made the boys put out their cigarettes under their heels on the floor, walk to the wall across from them, and invite the girls who had been eyeballing them to dance, so they could all get in a double line, facing each other in order to coordinate their collective body. The majority sang out *She loves you, yeah, yeah, yeah* and moved their heads back and forth.

At some point on that double, twisting line danced Alfredo and, in front of him, a real Adela, smiling, following the bouncing ball and swimming, undulating in the middle of an afternoon that was turning into night, and if Freddy were ever to make up his mind, she would end up warming her hand with his, and then they would give each other a real kiss, not like the ones she gave him at the highest point of his daydreams. No, he had her now, looking at her with eyes full of desire, hoping that they would play *Ana* and he would find himself closer to her and tell her things that he had never told her before. After several songs, they didn't play *Ana*, but in its place rang out *I'll Return* and it was all the same because with professional spins Adela and Freddy pressed their cheeks together and, so that no one else could hear them talking, they began to love each other amid the Beatlemania that they had just discovered.

Many of the romances of that era began at those afternoon parties. You kissed the person you really wanted to kiss, but what did it matter if you also kissed the person that you really loved. Babies were conceived that we were dreaming about having years later. At these parties no one imagined that fifteen years later many of those dancers would be going in and coming out of offices, with a couple of kids in tow, only to turn around and go home, a little tired and, put on a record by *The Beatles* just because, in some way, they kept on loving them in a melancholy way, and the five-year-old child, a blatant fanatic of *The Beatles* and *The Rolling Stones*, is told that, yes, one is John Lennon, the other one Paul McCartney, and this one here is George Harrison, and the drummer is Ringo Starr.

free time

Every morning I buy a newspaper and every morning, as I read it, my fingers become smeared with ink. It has never bothered me to get them dirty, so long as I keep up to date on all the news. But this morning, when I picked up the paper, I felt extremely ill. I thought that it was just a matter of one of my frequent dizzy spells. I paid for the paper and returned home. My wife had gone shopping. I settled into my favorite chair, lit a cigarette, and began reading the first page. Immediately after learning that a jet had crashed, I started feeling sick again. I looked at my fingers and found them dirtier than usual. Overcome by a tremendous headache, I went to the bathroom, calmly washed my hands, and now less shaken, returned to my chair. When I reached for my cigarette, I discovered a black stain covering my fingers. Hurriedly I returned to the bathroom and scrubbed my hands with a bristle pad and a pumice stone. Finally I washed with bleach but it was useless because the stain had grown and spread all the way to my elbows. More worried than angry now, I called the doctor and he recommended that I take an extended vacation or a long nap. Later on I called the newspaper office to register the most scathing complaint. The woman who answered the phone merely insulted me and treated me as though I were crazy. While I was talking on the phone, I realized it wasn't a stain at all, but rather an infinite number of tiny letters tightly packed together, like a swarming multitude of black ants. When I hung up the little letters had reached my waist. In alarm, I ran to the front door; but before I could open it my legs gave out from under me and I fell to the floor with a crash. Flat on my back I discovered that, besides the large number of ant-letters that now covered my entire body, there were also a few photographs. I lay there for several hours until I heard the door open. I had difficulty forming the thought, but finally I was convinced that I had been saved. My wife came in, picked me up from the floor, tucked me under her arm, settled into my favorite chair, thumbed through me casually, and began to read.

story with a jacaranda

for Russell M. Cluff

Several years ago the change of seasons took on an incomprehensible nature, especially the painful mutation from winter to spring. That is what was happening during the first days of April. Sudden heat waves alternated with violent, forceful winds and slight breezes that were accompanied by an intense, cutting cold. After being pounded by highs and lows and turbulence, the climate began to stabilize and was smothered in a monotony that subtly arouses one's desire.

Despite the construction going on everywhere and the enormous amount of space covered by concrete, vegetation was spreading throughout the city. In some areas it was merely evident through tiny garden plots, precarious tin cans, or a few trees on the sidewalks. But, to the west vegetation was taking over the wide streets. It stopped at the edge of the extensive gardens by the houses, climbed the walls, and sprang toward the sidewalks like green and blue rivers and bougainvilleas.

Outside one of these estates, in Lomas of Chapultepec, a man of modest dress stood beneath a large jacaranda. He was admiring its great violet canopy, seemingly tattered. He gaged its height, imagining the thunderous din and the spectacular sight that the tree would cause if it came crashing down on the street. It might reach the other curb and even kiss the wall of the opposite house. Many times he had watched it turn green, violet and then back to sepia.

It was the tree he prized the most. Periodically he would prune the dead ends, and snip off shoots that could go wild. He would spray it, and paint its trunk every time it got skinned. He did all this because this was one of the largest, most beautiful jacarandas in the area, and because it was Angela's tree. As had happened many times that morning, people stopped to look at it in bloom. The praise he overheard from passersby was one of his most important rewards, just like Angela's exaggerated exclamations. A word dropped here or there made him feel as though his existence was meaningful despite his beat up work shoes and denim pants, his heavy red and white checkered work shirt and his baseball cap.

The man lowered his eyes, adjusted his cap, turned to his right, and headed for the half-open wrought-iron gate. He opened, closed it behind him, ready to execute the order. The large black double doors were joined on the east to a high fence, and together they formed a front of about forty meters. The black snakes of the wrought-iron climbed in spirals and ended in spearheads pointing toward the sky. The joints, where the snakes of the fence and the gate came together, were hidden by a laminated white sunflower. The succession of heads formed half moons standing on end.

The large two-story house, its walls painted oyster white against the black iron work, was located about thirty meters back from the street; in between were many plants and a few strategically placed trees. A double row of bushes lined the straight road that divided the large garden in half. Down this lane walked the man with the baseball cap. He nearly reached the main door when he turned to the right, then he disappeared behind several mock apple bushes. The rectilinear windows were indicative of a discreet, precise, and sober architecture that contrasted with the wrought-iron work along the street.

When the man entered, Angela watched him from her top floor window, until he was lost from view. She looked for a moment at the violet jacaranda flowers, fluttering above the fence. She looked at them as if wishing to freeze them in time. Then she turned away, and rounding the bed she headed for the closet. She began taking out her clothes, arranging them on the cherry red and gold Gobelino bedspread.

Angela was a tall, thin, pretty woman. Her black hair caressed the half-moons of her neck and shoulders, and her complexion was more fair than dark. The slight rings under her gray eyes faded into her barely noticeable cheeks. A straight but strong nose, a mouth with full lips. Full breasts suggestive and ample. A thin waist, mature hips, long legs. Angela was twenty-six years old. A burning sensation began to overwhelm her sense of calm as she continued arranging her clothes. She thought that this time she would not cry.

From the moment she left the table on the first floor, after a long silence following her words to the attorney, Humberto Mateos L., she promised herself she would not cry. Before going downstairs, Angela had decided that, come what may, she would not get up until the last ritual involving her in that house was over. Her steadfastness came from a special understanding that permeated body and soul and was full of contradictory sentiments, but seeing her path for the first time clearly and definitively. Sadness, dizziness, hate, pity, affection, suddenly came together. Beneath this diversity of sensations lurked anguish and fear—hard, dry, painful—she could not deny them nor did she wish to, since they too had a part to play. On other occasions when she had tried to leave home she had failed, immersing herself in a similar spiritual multiplicity. Threats, blackmail, doubt, blame, tears, had made her unpack her bags, and she accepted the rewards that failure provided her. Last night's scene had paved her way, unchained her emotions and persuaded her irrevocable action.

At three in the morning, Luis Arturo parked the Mercedes Benz alongside the jacaranda. Angela noticed that the light was on in the first floor library. Nervous, she still spent another half hour with Luis Arturo. The purpose of their conversation wasn't that important. At last she said good night to him, got out of the car, opened the gate, and crossed somewhat hurriedly through the shadows of the garden, feeling the cold wind on her face and hands. She entered by the front door, heading for the staircase in darkness. After going up and walking nervously to her bedroom, Humberto Mateos stuck his head out of the library and called to her.

Though she felt like ignoring him, the woman obeyed. After she entered the library, he closed the door calmly. Without saying a word, the man approached the olive green velvet sofa in front of him. He picked up a quiver that contained five razor-sharp arrows and hung it over his right shoulder. Then he took a red bow, rested it on the floor, and applied pressure from top to bottom, curving the wood. He fixed the string in the groove. It vibrated like the string of a cello. His movements were skillful, rapid, exact. He placed an orange-colored arrow on the string, aimed it toward the book stand full of large volumes, then turned slowly, fixing on the back of the chair near Angela. It appeared he had found the target where he would shoot the arrow, but suddenly he dropped his arms and replaced the arrow in the quiver. He looked into the woman's gray eyes and in a brusque, tense voice, still pretending to be calm, he said: "Come, follow me."

They left the library and descended into the darkness of the garden. The woman, stunned, followed the man, overcome by sheer terror, without an inkling as to what was happening. At the moment when she supposed Mateos would shoot, her feelings were clouded by a murky veil that distanced her from these events, and she followed the man just to be following him. Mateos turned to the left toward the tool shed, next to a large doghouse. Suddenly the lights came on, revealing greenish blue, reddish green or greenish yellow splotches moving rhythmically in the wind. They heard muffled barking. The man appeared, pulling a young dalmatian on a chain. They moved with difficulty into the grass a few meters from the woman. He attached the chain to the trunk of a glossy privet tree and disappeared. Mateos chose an arrow with a razor-sharp point and placed it carefully on the string. He raised his arms, forming a triangle over the base of the half moon of the bow, aiming at the animal. The dog barked and growled without stopping. He tried to escape by tugging violently on the chain. The spots on the map of his skin flashed intermittently because of his movements in the light. He pointed his long snout toward his owner, his moist eyes seemed perplexed, unable to understand what was happening. The scent of flowers reached the dog's nose, and Angela also tried to find an answer in the aromas of the night. Perhaps all the dog's senses had created that instinctive and conditioned recollection about the use of the weapon that at that moment was aimed at him and not at the animals he had retrieved and placed with precision at Mateos' feet.

In the cold air of that early April dawn, slicing through the smells and the night, the arrow, a shaft of light, whistled, flying almost invisibly like tenuous lightning, penetrating the tense muscles of the dalmatian's neck. The dog's body fell heavily backwards, as if a solid kick of a foot had knocked him down forever. A few strange sounds came from his throat and he quivered as his blood stained the grass. "One of the best archers in the country," the man said. Then, there was only silence.

Angela ran into the house, went up to her bedroom, and locked herself in. For a long time she heard noises coming from the garden, noticing through the darkness that the light outside was fading. She heard the man's movements upstairs, and she knew that he also had gone into his bedroom. Only then was she able to breathe normally. She took off her shoes and began pacing the floor. "If I could leave at this moment I would," was the first thought that entered the woman's mind. Precious little of the night was left.

Angela went to bed without undressing. With her eyes closed she relived portions of her recollections that overlapped one another. She reviewed her previous attempts to leave home. Distant voices, scenes, colors, faces superimposed themselves until she recalled the night when her mother, looking as young as the day she died, woke her up and said, "Sweetheart, Sweetheart, come, get up." Without understanding, the child obeyed and saw the grief and urgency on her mother's face. She dressed her only in a coat and together they hurriedly left the apartment. As they were descending the stairs, the child asked: "And Daddy, Mommy?" The young mother said nothing and picked the child up before going out into the street. A car was waiting for them outside.

After that recollection was repeated several times, always without providing any answers, Angela began to calm down, and with the brightness of the sunrise she fell asleep. She awakened at mid-morning, bathed and dressed, made a few phone calls, and went down for breakfast. The attorney, Humberto Mateos L., was spreading butter on his toast. Angela sat down across from him. She looked at his balding head, his reddish nose, the honey-colored suede hunting vest. An Indian woman dressed in a white and pink striped uniform served them in silence.

After orange juice, after a few sips of black coffee, Angela spoke: "Daddy, I'm leaving." The man tried to say something, but she cut him off: "I don't want to hear it. There is absolutely nothing to discuss." Mateos understood, and refrained from saying anything. But he ordered the servant to call Celorio. Minutes later, Celorio appeared turning his baseball cap round and round in his hands. "Good morning," he said without looking at either the man or the woman, "what would you like me to do, Don Humberto?" "I want you to cut down the jacaranda tree by the street." Noticing that Celorio did not move, he repeated: "Go chop it down with the axe . . . Now, did you understand?" "Yes, Don Humberto," he answered and left, putting his cap back on.

bluesy morning

Cristina gets up. Crap, like I'm beat. Cristina feels terrible, bleary-eyed. Crap, like it's Saturday and I'm really beat. The party was kickin', a blow-out. Real hot, you dig? You wanna have a rum and Coke or maybe a joint? The deal was that I was smashed out of my mind. That night, after the blow-out, Cristina slept in her clothes; now she has to get undressed at ten a.m. and get dressed again at ten-thirty or, if she hurries, maybe by a quarter after. The good thing is I've got some real cool clothes, man; all you've got to do is sniff them out in the discount stores or at the open-air markets. They said I wouldn't put on the tight stuff, but like Yola couldn't handle it, and she said I was trying to look like real hot stuff, like ya know? And Cristina undresses, she takes off her tight, faded, denim jeans with the doubly wide cuff and her silky coffee-colored blouse. I can't handle the feel of a bra, no way. I don't know, I guess ya gotta break with your old lady's rags, and when I can get away with it, not even panties. She puts on an old yellow robe that totally transforms her. Cristina mixes a rum and Coke; one cuba she can handle, even two, but little-bitty ones. She likes getting a buzz, but not letting it get out of hand, she's wild but she takes care of herself, because at a blow-out you never know what could happen to you, and there is always some dork that wants to stick it to you. Cristina comes out of the bedroom pushing aside the curtain that serves as a door. She walks barefoot and the cold cement really pisses her off. Everyone's up, but she could care less. Cristina goes into the bathroom, there she takes off the robe and her panties that she just happened to put on yesterday. Her tan-colored skin is smooth, real smooth, without a tummy, no love handles. A cold shower brings back her natural beauty, tenses her muscles, gives her that hot look. Like I'm not into sports anymore, that's little girl shit. All that crap about wearing shorts bit, screw it, what a bunch of bullshit, got it? Yeah, yeah, I groove on dancing. I don't know, like it's music that really gets to ya. Then Yola, like don't be a retard, girl. And Cristina, so I'm not saying that you shouldn't play Rigo Tovar, like he's really hot, no question. Like, right on. A little cold-water bath—there's no other way because no one's going to fire up the boiler—and life returns to that new bod. She comes out of the shower and has to dry off with a wet towel, already used that morning by everyone in the house, but she doesn't even notice. She puts the robe back on and, as she leaves the bathroom, she hears her mom yell to her from the kitchen: What time did you get in? Cristina says "no way" under her breath and, without answering, goes back into her bedroom. She takes off the robe and lets it fly wherever and, while she puts on the green stick deodorant, naked, showing her tummyless tummy, sporting an athletic body without even trying, she tries out a few dance steps in her bedroom and, well—aren't you going to eat breakfast?—but Cristina dances a few more licks in the nude with all her sophomoric sixteen years to the warm air of midday, without a thought for the cold floor. She remembers the flute's soft lead in the dance melody and how at the dance its flute's notes were extraordinarily mesmerizing. Cristina dancing through the night, Cristina dancing in the morning, always to the strains of an imaginary dance tune: this next one that's ringing in her head, and yesterday's that from the speakers next to her legs transformed her into someone else, that is if you listen to it with all you've got, it sounds different, it moves you, you hear what I'm saying?

When she goes through the rickety wardrobe her father bought a long time ago in Monte de Piedad, she takes out a black cap that she had planned to wear since the day before yesterday to the blues concert and now with her athletic body and a black cap she can really boogie—a Maoist cap, provocatively Maoist, defiant because other chicks hassle her about dressing that way, they just aren't with it. What a bummer, ya know? After the second cuba I got a little tight, and I started sayin' all kinds of crap and I went and danced by myself. While Cristina was dancing alone, Felipe came up to her in his black denim vest and cream-colored boots, bought, of course, at *Canadá,* this is where it's at, and while he dances with Solitary Cristina he shows off the peach fuzz on his chest, athletic, no thanks to any of his efforts, uncovered peach fuzz, but Solitary Cristina doesn't even see Felipe dancing with her but she hears him say you're too cool, babe. Solitary Cristina hates his guts, kiss off, dude.

This time I won't put on any panties, because this concert is worth it. She slips into some tight white jeans that definitely show the line and hug those tight contours, Cristinaly athletic. She lays the cap on the gray rumpled sheets, drys her hair, her breasts rise and fall with her arms, the towel alternately hides and reveals Cristina's face. The black shirt has been ironed since yesterday. Felipe retorts, what a bummer, man. Come on, we dance real groovy, let's get it on and Cristina, no way, man, buzz off.

Cristina in her white jeans laughs in front of the bathroom mirror, remembering last night's blow-out, and the crimson eye shadow lights up her eyes and the mascara sparkles on her eyelashes. Last night when they dropped her off, Yola told her not to sleep in too late because the concert was at twelve and, just remember that at the *Ferrocarrilero* you were out of it. Before opening the door, Cristina said don't start bitching at me, because she'd be up on time. Cristina puts on her shirt, ties it in front, and under the cloth only firm little tits, unhindered, although small, breasts like tiny volcanoes. She eats breakfast with her hat on; a few black locks dangle beneath the brim. In great gulps she downs a cup of *café con leche*, devouring her sweet roll in three bites. Yola will be here any minute.

And that's true because just as Cristina wipes her mouth with a paper napkin, someone knocks at the door and when one of her little brothers opens it, she hears them ask for Cristi. She's up like a shot, come on in, she shouts, I'm ready and Yola comes in, ravishing. She's wearing a loose cherry-colored blouse, flowing wide sleeves, tight black denim jeans, very tight around the ankles, she has on black, spiked high-heeled shoes. Move it, O.K.? And Cristina moves it. With slippers flopping, she runs to her room; off come the slippers and from under the bed come some black, spiked high heels. She returns, and we're out of here, and they head for the dusty street, full of potholes; two blocks away they take the first bus and forty-five minutes later, at the intersection of University Avenue, the second, that will take them to the *Nezahualcóyotl Concert Hall*. Did you wake up with a hangover? Yola asks. And Cristina: Oh, I didn't go down on it too hard, I just got a little stoned. But Yola: Boy, I sure did, but I've already downed a beer. Who was playing that cool music? I don't know, Cristina answers, but that flute was way out; I wanted to dance alone but some dude kept hasslin' me. And Yola, well I got into it with a guy who wanted to lay me, but I told him no way José and he said what a prick tease and I answered you're the prick, like you want it for free; when I'm ready I'll have someone call ya, pal, but he kept pushin' me, lighten up, and I lightened up and right there he started feelin' me up. So we split. You were out of it, right?

They come to the *Nezahualcóyotl* stop and from there to the concert hall it's no more than a quick toke away. Take a big drag, another drag, suuusuuusuuus, and it was like they were competing to see who could suck the weed the loudest, sssss, ummmmm, out of sight, and when they reach the parking lot they douse it. They were all but airborne. Some guys, hey have you got an extra ticket, teach, lil' sisters, and already inside the hall, they hear a faint lead guitar, I told you so, it's already started. Bummer. There aren't any seats. I told you. Flipped out because of the multi-colored lights and strobes on the stage, they stop talking, they descend one of the lateral stairways hearing the applause of the crowd that follows the black voice of Willie Dixon and the drums and the bass and the lead guitar and the harmonica. They're dwarfed, they're almost blown away, but only for a moment, because soon they're swallowed up by the collective frenzy. They sit on the stairs and start smoking their *Baronets*, unconcerned, except for enjoying the music that they couldn't have imagined would be so totally out-of-sight and as if in unison they rise to their feet and soon begin to move their hips, while the blues continue and lick them unabashedly and they both close their eyes and let it all hang out. Their hips move more and more rapidly and the blues of the black night rocks the hall and at that moment only Willie Dixon exists, singing before an unfamiliar audience that seems to understand instinctively what they have come all the way from Memphis to perform.

Differences disappear while listening to that music that seems to be the invention of a happy, playful, persecuted god, and it brings out your sensibilities from among the sentimental wreckage that this sleazy society has brought out in you, right? And they seem to be serious musicians—even though each one dresses as he wishes—because they sweat, and join in to play a type of blues that sounds more like rock, and what is really outstanding, according to the program, Willie Dixon is over fifty years old and not a soul here is over thirty or under fifteen. And yet, Dixon understands what is happening to us and what turns us on, he wakes us up and with his thick, stumbling body he invites us to be happy and even though they brought him a Mexican hat he said he'd rather wear his, the one he bought in New York, because I'm not a clown, understand that I die a little each time I sing, I'm carrying around a plastic leg, I just like to see you enjoy yourselves because one way or another you young people today have been screwed over and I'm inviting you, my young friends, to let yourselves be seduced by these musicians who accompany me, and listen to the skill and sadness of Sunny Land Slim's piano, while my voice, I know it's hoarse and violent and happy, exudes a wild energy because our music is a strangely human mixture of yearnings for living, crying, shouting, loving, all just beyond our grasp and it's great that you make a scene and interrupt me and howl because without you everything would be so sad—this empty hall with the sad melody of ghostly blues would kill me—but the good thing is that you are here and you come up close and you don't pay any attention to the guards when they tell you to be polite and sit down.

Everything's just fine; now listen to this rock song that you remember from the *Rolling Stones* and get all worked up and we'll get all worked up and we'll all want to dance in the hall, but no, only a handful of girls swing their hips in their tight jeans and dance on their way down and are joined by those rude guys who have never set foot in *Nezahualcóyotl* before and who, when they start jostling around in front of the stage, desecrate the concert hall and transform it, for two eternal hours, into a hole, a blues hole, a funky hole, while Willie Dixon says he likes *the little Mexican girls* and they understand and nod their heads and one girl drops her black cap and she doesn't even care, please, sit down, you're getting in the way, stick it, man, suuusuuusuuusss and the whole place fills with voluptuous smoke, suuusuuusuuussssss, and then they swing their hips, above all their hips, because the concert is worth it and us old guys, turkeys, philosophers, pin heads, writers, awesome dudes, press, long-haired kids, rockers, bros, doctors, hoodlums, engineers, sociologists, flower children, go wild at the first blues festival in Mexico and we can't hold still because they have never let the *Beatles*, the *Rolling Stones*, *Yes*, or *Genesis*, anybody, come, and now that the flashy John Lee Hooker shows up who cares if the *Nezahualcóyotl Concert Hall* is turned into a blues dive with greenishorangishbluishreddish lights and if they don't want us to smoke because, what the hell, man, ya have to enjoy and we're enjoying, we, the ten thousand kids who submerge ourselves in blues that groan, demand, free our emotions because the blues are here and, even though the years have passed, the spirit of the old blues singers is rejuvenated in the melody and, under their Panama hats demanding the right to be me, an individual, a person who decides for himself, they force you to respect them.

And, like a euphoric gift, the kids bunched up down in front begin to roll like a wheel and, in the middle of it, as if sprouting from the yearnings of all the people, a black man dances, moving sensuously, while John Lee Hooker shoots off his guitar seated on an *ad hoc* chair, moving only his fingers, the trigger of the guitar, and staring impassively at the kids who shout for him to come closer, he agrees and stands and now there are two black men dancing, one slowly, the one down below surrounded by kids, and that damned Lee, letting it all hang out, who keeps on machine gunning our minds in order to close the entire, supreme cycle, soul brother, and the whole place turns into swaying arms following in the air the sound of the harmonica that is about to disintegrate in the big mouth of that poorly dressed blueser and the music continues and the music goes on and the blues continue, Big Walter Horton's harmonica plays on and sure, they're foreign names, they're men from other galaxies, but it's as if someone said

Rodríguez or Aguilar because they love us with their harmonicas and with their three hundred guitars, and they transmit a lifelong experience of nights and mornings to us and they're tearing themselves open in a song that lasts five minutes because five minutes are enough to tear open an entire life and that's why we sway and howl, admiring the traditional and nostalgic guitar of Jimmy Rogers, man, and then, what?, if that's what we want, no way, there's nothin' more to say, it would have been better for the entire Federal District to learn by personal experience what four musicians on stage are capable of, standing up there as if it were nothing, as if they had just come from home, here, two blocks away, after breakfast and all of us, audience and musicians, have forgotten that outside the hall there is sun and clouds and a city that grows spasmodically with its violence, and inside the hall, it hits me, another sun has risen, the sun of the blues, my friends, have them come out and play the last number and the screaming is even louder, John Lee Hooker refuses, but the stomping, the applause, the shouting, the whistling demand it, he leaves, he's tired of shining his sun for this Mexican public, nevertheless John Lee Hooker gives in and the door through which he left opens and the pandemonium is indescribable, we'll have to keep the memory of it under our skin forever, with the voice of Willie Dixon tattooed on our arms like a tarantula and the wild eyes of that damned Lee encased in some corner of this collective body, and the uproar becomes indescribable because Lee Hooker agrees to continue machine gunning us and he asks with his provocative presence if we want him to keep on shooting us, if we want the sun to keep shining inside the hall, and we tell him yes with our applause, howling, shouting and waving of arms and hips. The hall grows mysteriously quiet, it waits for the equipment to be turned on again and then a guitar begins playing the final notes of the morning.

dr. mane

for Esther Harari

Polish the style, choose and string together phrases.

Ah, old observer of caterpillars!

Li Ho (trans. by Marcela de Juan)

. . . *Scurrilous bitch, mangy poetry* . . .

José Emilio Pacheco

It was the first autumn night, a clear sky, millions of stars at around two o'clock in the morning. Perhaps of all the windows of the building, those on the first floor were the only ones lit. Behind those windows was my house and, in the back, my study, and I was in it, organizing my shelves and files. I had spent virtually the entire day doing that job that requires attention at least once a week. I confess that a large part of the time was spent rereading letters, poems, notes, unsalvageable stories, and a whole pile of memos and papers that I'm in the habit of collecting. Enjoying myself, I was happily reading a jabberwocky poem (unpublishable, of course), when I heard several knocks at my window. The window faces the garden that I water daily but which belongs to all of the tenants of the building. It was strange that, even though the lights of the house were off, someone should be knocking on the window in the wee hours of the morning. I opened the curtain (still feeling in my smile the flutter of the absurd images of the last verse) and found myself facing Dr. Mane. The doctor was given that name because of the way he looks on his drinking days; in fact, even though he has never worn long hair (his medical profession will not permit it), you might say that he does have unruly hair that would remind you of bristly poems bursting into the air, a useless comb, Medea transforming herself into Dr. Mane. When I saw him, I gestured to him by joining my thumb and forefinger, indicating that I would let him in in just a minute. I left the study, walked down the hall, and turned to the right through the dining room, straight to the front door and opened it. Blurting out some sort of greeting (it probably was a greeting), Dr. Mane entered. He was wearing a dull black suit, tight pants, a short dress coat, a large collar, a tie, a Napoleon III style beard, and distinctive sideburns; he was a man of about thirty-five rugged years, dark. I all but dragged him into the living room, all but forcibly seated him in the easy chair he liked so much, and all but lit and smoked his cigarette for him. If he hadn't said, "This apartment is too cold," as he walked through the open door, as was his congenial custom, it would have meant that things weren't going all that well with him. On several occasions I had seen him depressed, for it won't be denied that he was given to these moods. Nevertheless, on that night of the jabberwockies, his depression demanded distance, thought, a great deal of tact, moments of silence, understanding, a glass of liquor, soft-spoken words, perhaps an arm around his shoulders. Before taking any initiative, I stopped in front of him in the middle of the living room, to observe him carefully without asking any questions, hoping that he would begin the conversation. While I was watching him I imagined that he had lost one of his patients during surgery.

I lit a cigarette. With the smoke from the first puff I blew out the match. The smoke followed a descending path, dropping until it disappeared into Dr. Mane's hair. He was resting his elbows on his thighs, his fingers intertwined and his gaze riveted on his knobby fingers. His posture did not permit me to see his sideburn-covered face, which might indicate some justification for his presence in my living room. His mane stood erect, wolf-like, hermetic, dark, and somewhat silvery, with millions of bristles exploding against the back of the easy chair like a hoary blotch of ink; wizard hair, cryptic, mystagogical, but also promontory, ashen and dusty with future words, sad, friendly. I consented to prolong the silence. Intuitively I knew we needed a drink. I went to the portable bar and took out two glasses. In one I poured whiskey; in the other, tequila. I brought them to wizard hair and I offered Mane the one with whiskey. He unclenched his fingers and, before taking the glass, he looked at me as if wishing to say: "You guessed it, right? You knew that it would all end this way, that Textófaga would push me aside in order to perform this unworthy and desperate act, that worm, that violet dragon little by little would surround me; that after the very last verse, not only would she enter into the broad territory and into the voice—extended feather—empty space—aspirated page, the place where the cracks disappear and the key is a mouth without a tongue, but rather also the trembling typewriter, the abuse of step-parents, the smiling dragon, the door-knob of the traveling door, offering itself to me in a childish manner, naked doorknob, counterfeit striptease, a mute iron viper. The same old story, right?"

At last he grabbed the glass, he drank slowly. I followed his rhythm; I had the entire autumn night to soak up his sorrow; I could listen to him until daybreak. I went to the kitchen, opened the refrigerator, took out a lime and sliced it; I took the salt shaker from the cupboard and put it on the tray together with the lime slices. Every sound was hideous: the opening and shutting of the front door, Dr. Mane's footsteps, the drinks splashing into the glasses, the scratching of a match across its box, the exhale of smoke, the swallowing of a drink, the refrigerator door closing, the knife slicing limes, the salt shaker being placed on the platter, the sound of my shoes upon the kitchen and living room floors, and my vigorous sucking on a slice of lime in front of the mystagogical hair, and even the rustling of the doctor's coat when he held out his arm with an empty glass, signaling that I should refill it. All these sounds on the first floor of our building were far too loud.

After the first swallow of his second whiskey, Mane fidgeted in his easy chair, his tongue appearing time and again between his lips. Mane fixed his eyes upon mine.

"I hanged him. I couldn't stand it any more and I hanged him," he said with a calm voice that showed fatigue, perhaps a savage calm. "You were witness to the treatment that I gave him, you yourself collaborated with us so that everything would be secretive and turn out perfectly. You remember that I came daily to talk to you about it, to discuss with you every detail of the process. And now the moments of euphoria and happiness come back to me. You can't believe what a strange and pleasant sensation overcame me when I saw the precise rhythm of this thing and its unrivaled structure; at that point I was the happiest physician in the world. However, I was awakened by a troubling dream, a poorly projected shadow, a scoffing face on the bus, a word written by itself and dancing alone in the air, a surprising headache, the snorting of the violet dragon, or the voices pounding in my brain—any one of these facts immersed me in doubt and I had to start all over, around and around the zero, that damned number with which I have always struggled and that has never been more than a shackle binding me to despair, to uneasiness, to fear, to paranoid gossip, to intimate belittlement, concealing me, separating me from my patient, forever walking down dark passageways, smiling grotesquely when surprised by one of Textófaga's faces, hurriedly leaving the subway, precipitously opening the door to my apartment and installing bars and dark curtains on the windows. No, it was not possible to continue in that manner, surrounded by time's anxiety, awakening with that dark sensation that caused me to see a totally distorted world, a world much longer than all of those black passageways linked together, putting up with the divine delinquency of Textófaga, for whom no laws exist, much less a tribunal in which to reconcile each house search, which she cynically executes. The only truth left to me now is that I hanged him. I hanged him and the very mention of it hurts so much. But, perhaps, that was the most practical solution for everyone. I still remember the shadow of his legs projected by the chandelier where I hanged him; they swayed in a most sinister way against the north wall of my study and, although inverted, a few words could still be distinguished, shadowy words, agonizing words; one of the most vile verbs dangled horribly from his purple lips. I'll never forget the scene . . .

Silence possessed Dr. Mane, his gaze was nailed to the hardwood floor; once more the glass of whiskey in his hand traveled to his lips. I went over to the sofa, I put a dash of salt on my lime, I sucked on it and, before sitting down, I ruffled the doctor's mane even more. I had the urge to embrace him and kiss him and make love to him. To give my body to him as a substitute for the one he had murdered. But I knew that any approach on my part was forbidden because Dr. Mane had made a lifelong decision and any consoling utterance from me would be out of place. I felt impotent, beaten, uneasy. But soon hatred began to overpower me. I hadn't been wrong in considering an action similar to the one the doctor had confessed. Textófaga, the violet dragon, was mixed up in all this dirty business. I knew it. That divine calamity, with whom I have had to contend on innumerable occasions, had triumphed once again. That goddess who calmly sips cappuccino coffee in the cafeteria and goes to the movies only to return later to her infernal typewriter; she wanders in disguise through cocktail parties and exhibits with no one being the wiser; she puts her arm around your shoulder, or she rejects your greeting when you offer her the brightest of all your smiles, she gets drunk, whistles, is the earthiest of all mortals, outliving all of them. Textófaga dances, sleeps in many of our beds, listens to classical music, rock, jazz or blues, Latin music, she sodomizes and beats us, she's a thousand beings: a dragon with four thousand shaking female heads—foxes, asses, lynxes, crows and sows—she promotes, revises, critiques, dissects, instigates polemics on any available blank page. Textófaga sleeps, vomits, she brushes our teeth; Textófaga defecates and tenderly provides antidiarrhetics, she kisses us, eats cake in the morning with us, borrows our books and never returns them, swallows, swallows, devours; mistress of the zero, she is our hands, our dictionary of synonyms, our lame language, she carries a sword and a scarlet cape, she speaks all languages, she is the Altamira dragon. Many are the calamities that she has strewn along our paths, and not only does she attack, devour, burn, whisper, spread gossip, defame, and invent out-and-out riots, but she also belittles, oppresses with the force of four thousand silent mouths, leaves the pages blank; mother of errata, she demands to be called THE GREAT PROPRIETOR OF THE PARTS (and of the wholes). Among her four thousand heads, only one hundred have eyes; they are the redemptive heads, they spew forth a fire of letters from their angelical retinas. She has the gift of invading bodies, she passes through walls and spies through windows, she gnaws at hearts and lungs, she comfortably resides in one's very core. She knows what you are writing and what you will write, she causes books to vanish, she breaks inkwells, she hides contributions that are about to be published, she calls you on the telephone, she pulverizes the graphite of your pencils, she shaves you in the morning and drinks your orange juice . . .

I knew that both of us, Dr. Mane and I, had the same thoughts. Of course we had them. Furthermore, it served the purpose of expelling the whirlwind of images that welled up in our oral cavities. While I drank a little more tequila, I remembered the most spectacular event perpetrated by Textófaga against Mane. The doctor left for a week of vacation, sufficient time for him to rest and for her to perform the divine calamity. Anticipating an attack by Textófaga, Mane had two locks put on the door of his apartment. No one could come in through the windows due to the thick iron grating that covered them. The book of poems that the doctor had been writing for more than five years had been hidden in one of the legs of his bed, hollowed out *ex profeso*. Hoping to distract the goddess, he placed several poems on his desk. When he returned from his trip, all tanned, Dr. Mane immediately realized that Textófaga had made a visit. To begin with, he found the entryway door sprung, the hinges twisted. The locks had disappeared. According to the story he told me, at that moment he felt like screaming louder than he ever had in his entire life. The apartment was in a shambles, books were strewn all over the floor, paintings and papers were torn, curtains were shredded, the closet was ruined, the doctor's clothes were scattered throughout the room; in essence, it looked as though a tornado had leveled the apartment (Mane saw teeth marks in the wood of his desk top). But what bothered him the most was that his bed was upside down and, of course, the hiding place in the leg was more hollow than ever. Little by little, nervous and frightened, Mane began to gather his most beloved objects. Slowly, tears of rage welled up in his eyes, and little by little he approached his desk where, besides teeth marks, he discovered his book of poems and a note that read more or less like this:

Dear Gastroenterologist:

I was already acquainted with the poems you left out. They're terrible. That's why you used them for bait. It would have been easier for both of us if you had left me the little book, because you can see what happened. You only made me more angry. I realize your genius in hiding manuscripts; but it would be nice if you were to use it in your poetry. I read your poems very carefully; they aren't bad, but they're not very good. Several of the sonnets have an abominable cadence; the metaphors resemble overflowing bedpans. The poems in free verse are the worst.

I would like you to review the annotations that I took the liberty of making on the original (I congratulate you: it is well typed). Don't consider me your enemy, extend me your hand of friendship. Let me recommend that you stop neglecting your patients so much.

Affectionately, T.

P.S. The gratings on your windows are really ridiculous.

Before cleaning up the apartment, Dr. Mane began checking Textófaga's corrections. It was really a pity: the manuscript was in the same condition as the apartment. From that day on Mane decided to pay much more attention to his book of poems; he simply had to triumph over the violet dragon. However, soon there would be other attacks from divine calamity. For example, after incorporating Textófaga's corrections, Mane presented a very rigorous selection (fifteen sonnets) to an independent publisher; the board of editors accepted it and even congratulated him. A week after receiving this news (which Mane celebrated at Garibaldi Square), he received a strange telegram stating: "Upon entering press text of original poems darkened blotched disappeared large title only each page: not to be published bad very bad. Editorial Board reverses decision." Later, the doctor submitted four epigrams to a literary supplement and, although they were published, a few verses had gone crazy with erroneous prepositions, looney typos, and Soviet typography. Another disaster. And I could mention many cases just likc this one, but the important thing is that this entire ominous process forced the doctor to come to the decision that he made that autumn night.

"I remembered something about my apartment . . . ," Mane said while massaging the ink stain on his head.

"I was also thinking about that . . . ," I said, serving myself another tequila.

"I still can't believe it," he added. "It seems almost like a ghost story, an absolute nightmare. I don't know, I'm completely beside myself. It's been three days now since I last slept and I don't know how many more still await me. At times, late at night, it's odd, a whole string of images come to me and the whole matter seems absurd, even ridiculous, or comical," Mane spoke as though his lips had a mind of their own, "or dramatic," in one lone burst of laughter. "I found myself in front of a rotary press printing my book, but suddenly I was distracted and the machine yanked me toward its innards until it sank its teeth into one arm and then the other and then my head and all my body and I heard some macabre sounds and then there was an accompanying, gloomy silence and the vision began with exactitude, relentless." Mane's lips continued moving by themselves, blurting out a robotic voice. "This very night, before coming here, I was tossing in my bed, sweating, desperate; upon the ceiling of my bedroom my writer friends began to parade before me, but their appearance was not that of intellectuals (very likely, Textófaga had possessed me), but rather they looked like stocking salesmen or successful shop keepers. . . . Look, when I started to write I wanted to be like Rimbaud, but the image in the mirror constantly brought me back to my infantile reality, and then it said to me: 'You look like a telegraph operator, not a poet. . . . ' It's likely that that contradiction fed the characters who appeared on the ceiling: waiters, basketball players, railroad workers, charlatans, Linotype operators, boatmen, pimps, mailmen. Each one of them was carrying a small placard on his forehead: Verlaine, Mailer, Joyce, Herodotus, Alberti, Wilde, and De Quincey. It's terrible, believe me, to have a brain like Terence and the mug of a happy-go-lucky baker, or to be convinced that our ideas are like those of Marcel Schwob and to look like a magician for children's parties. Of course, not all the images that crossed my ceiling were like these. Once in a while, an elegant, good looking artist pranced by, but these were in the minority, as if to demonstrate the ironic reality of the majority. After a poetess with the face of a bilingual secretary came by, I thought for the first time that I would have to hang it. The idea continued to grow with the passing of the hours, and with the continuous swallowing of the press; hang it, hang it, hang it, I repeated to myself in an obsessive manner. I spent more than seven years working on it and was still dissatisfied; I don't know where the assonance came from, the cacophony, misplaced accents, the metaphors like tiny overflowing chamber pots, just as Textófaga once told me. Immersed in a frantic and anguished frenzy of corrections, fearing the day that the book would circulate in the stores, knowing that I was handcuffed, married to that damned zero, pursued by the future worms from the innards of the book of poetry, with door barred ahead of time, unable to go out for a walk in the park or smile without the specter of fear, distrustful even of my servant girl who didn't know how to read, with my face like that of a telegraph operator or barber, with panic invading me at the possibility of losing my original, but with greater fear of making copies, now that Textófaga might get hold of one of them, until the moment arrived in which I couldn't sleep and absurdity appeared and the press and the characters and the idea of hanging the book of poetry, killing it in order to dedicate myself to my patients. And I did it, but I didn't dare murder it with my own hands. I had to perform the entire stupid ceremony: bring a rope, tie the slip knot, repugnantly contemplate the one hundred sonnets, grab the book by its defenseless arms, place its head in the noose, tighten the knot and hang it from the lamp at midnight. But here comes the worst: while it agonized and its parabolic eyes burst from their sockets, I still found an error, a run-on line like an abrupt waterfall that hung by its arms just like the final scoff at a telegraph operator who once desired to be a poet like Rimbaud . . . "

"I understand you, I really do," I said in a meaningless way, because Doctor Mane had already understood everything, even the details. "I have also suffered such mediocrity; I look more like a pen-pushing grocer than a story writer, although I've always wanted to rave like Roberto Arlt. Regarding your barbaric act tonight, it isn't new to me either. Not long ago, I secretly shot a book of stories, but for reasons slightly different from yours. One morning, while I was bathing Textófaga came into the bathroom without my realizing her presence. I was singing a bolero *a viva voche* and I heard something squeaking, as if someone were drawing hearts with arrows on a dirty windshield. I stopped singing, threw open the plastic shower curtain and I saw a horrendous dwarf who speedily ran from the bathroom. Instinctively I looked at the mirror and found a message that the dwarf had written in the fog covering the silver-coated glass. The message said the following: 'The book of stories that you're thinking about publishing is no more than a rehash of your last stories.' I finished bathing, I dressed calmly, I went to my brother's home to borrow his rifle, he lent it to me, I returned home, I took out the book from the false bottom of the closet (Textófaga had scribbled all over it to the point of lunacy), we went out into the garden, I wasn't about to hear any excuses, I leaned it against the east wall without covering its eyes, ready, aim, and I put seven cabalistic bullets through it. I buried it in that very spot, underneath an azalea bush. Since that lightning quick funeral, I decided to write something else. As you can see, my dear Mane, my case is different from yours. I murdered a book so that not only the blossoms of my azalea would sprout from it, but also new and significant stories. At no moment did I feel guilty, neither did I show cowardice; this world is not for the faint hearted, like you. And forgive me for telling you all this when the new light of day frolics upon the window and you need the charity of my friendship." After I had said all this, Doctor Mane raised his head and, enraged, looked me straight in the eye; I was unable to hold back the torrent of my words. "Don't misunderstand me, I find myself on the other side of the dark hallways and of zero; I swim the length of number one. You're a pitiful and frightened man. You're the epitome of the man who deserves to suffer two Calvaries at the same time, the typical victim of the violet dragon; you're a nobody, a coward, a no-account dimwit." Mane stood up quickly, without taking his eyes off me. His face became flushed; I could feel smoke billowing out of my nostrils and I continued. "Please realize, the problem was that you wished to invent poetry of the twenty-first century, when from the past Pessoa, Auden, Gorostiza, T. S. Eliot, Quevedo, Montale, Lautréamont, Catullus, Salinas, Paz weighted you down like elephants, and I won't continue the list because we could spend this entire new day citing names. Textófaga was right, she was always right; it's time for you to prescribe your eternal antibiotics and your syrups for laryngitis, to tend to your varicose veins and your emergency cases of peritonitis. Neither poet nor doctor nor telegraph operator nor barb . . . ," I was unable to finish the sentence because Mane jumped on top of me, he gave me such a blow to the side of my face that it knocked me to the floor. While Doctor Mane repeated the word 'shit' over and over through clenched teeth he began to kick me in the head, then in the ribs, then in the legs until he tired. He jumped on my body that by now was face down, he took my head and beat it against the floor several times.

When I thought I would lose consciousness, the doctor stopped beating me. He began to cry very softly, like an abandoned child. He stood up, finished his whiskey, wiped his nose with the forearm of his dull black dress coat, mumbled something, and left the house when the day was but a single flame burning my chest.

when touch becomes word

. . . perhaps there still remained enough light for you to look through tears at the pewter sky, the city.

Julio Cortázar, *Last Round*

Both glances, with their one-hundred-eighty-degree field of vision, furrow the fluid space of the living room and the hall until they come to rest on the impenetrable vertical lines that disappear into the ceiling. Door openings sketched on the walls; the frames are still. The door at the end of the dining room appears with its hinges exposed: iron butterflies sleeping on wood. Part of a kitchen the size of the door, incomplete metal figures: mutilated cupboards, half of a refrigerator. The eyes circle, bouncing from a table to a picture of a child with a lamb, only to be tossed out toward the emptiness of the living room. There, they bury themselves until they meet the wall in the hall where that glance spreads and penetrates momentarily into the cracks—the vulvae of the wall. They see the wood of five-and-a-half well worn steps. Her eyelids fall and seem to turn off the light in slow motion. Now, she sees only one hundred and eighty degrees of darkness, with a few insignificant streams of light mixed with somewhat opaque reds and greens. For him, doors, windows, kitchen, hallway, moldings, tables, butterflies, mutilation, lamb, stairs, vulvae; on the other hand, for her all this continues to exist, but outside her eyes, in the great beyond of her darkness. Only then do they realize that she is resting one foot on his legs and he one hand on that foot. She doesn't want to open her eyes; it's better to let them rest. Only touch and imagination, of course. Our silence was nothing special, something a little out of the ordinary, easily explained by our nervous silence. The noiseless house was the extraordinary thing and not extraordinary in a mysterious sense. The explanation was that ordinarily there are the sounds of children, the street, parents and of our own voices when we speak. Despite these very normal circumstances, we felt a little strange and a bit foreign to one another. At first when we had sat down on the sofa she put her two feet on my legs, but later only one remained, the left one. She let her other leg and foot fall, almost touching the floor with the tips of her toes. The dangling leg looked like something that didn't belong to her, an independent, lazy leg hanging from the couch. We forgot about that inert leg that had nothing to do with us, while noticing total solidarity in the other foot. I could feel its light pressure, I noticed the clothing that covered it: its shoe with a small hole in the heel; I could see her stocking as far up as the shin. The suede of the shoe felt a little cool, but as I cupped it in my hand it warmed up. The warmth had penetrated to the skin, and my girlfriend, enjoying it, closed her eyes to relish the energy that had filtered through her stocking.

When I slid my hand to the back of her foot, I found the heel naked of its shoe, but clothed in stocking. Upon feeling that my fingers had reached that crease, she was startled, wanting to withdraw her foot, showing genuine modesty. My hand held it there by applying a little pressure, since the resistance exerted by the foot was normal under such circumstances. I particularly enjoyed her bashfulness because a touch of modesty was necessary; perhaps if such a reaction had not existed the magic of the moment would have disappeared just like the other foot. Then I realized that she was not wearing just one stocking, but two. The inner one was smaller and its pale yellow color could be seen through the coarser weave of the outer one. In a moment of frenzy, the hand rapidly unloosed the strap. With great tenderness it went about taking off the shoe until the foot was covered only by stockings. Under the stockings, the toes moved ever so slightly; it could have signaled a reproach or merely an expression of pleasure. Now, the foot lay before the hand in its undergarments. It gave the impression of being somewhat defenseless, a condition that awakened certain yearnings in the hand, until it was overcome by an irregular trembling. The moment for heavy breathing had arrived and for wiping away several tiny drops of perspiration. The hand, with its nervous fingers, decided to caress the two small peaks that formed the ankle. Under the hand's caress it seemed that both tiny bones gave a start, appearing to swell, beginning to breathe. The fingers slid over the curve of the instep, as if gliding through snow, until they came to the toes. The hand enjoyed fondling them for a while and then moved back along the sole of the foot, stopping at the rear of the curvature: the heel. Here, not only did the fingers become involved, but, also, the palm of the hand. Now it covered all the roundness of that part. The thumb became blushed and active. Without a doubt it was totally aroused.

The foot was no longer thinking of anything except the embrace of the hand, sinking into this tender exchange. The hand, with a somewhat brusque movement, slid to the top of the stocking and modestly began removing it. As it slipped down, little by little the shin became exposed, displaying the glow of cleanliness itself. The right hand blushed slightly at seeing that the pale yellow stocking was no longer in view; but later when the foot was stripped of its outer stocking, the final covering was exposed which really was not another pale yellow full-length stocking, but rather a smaller yellowish sock that permitted the skin up to the calf to be exposed to the air. This stocking scarcely covered the blush of the small mounds on the ankle.

Neither the hand nor the foot could say where the bothersome full-length stocking had come to rest; obviously, that no longer interested them and they now found themselves decidedly involved in other things. At this point things began happening very fast. Unconsciously, one might say. The initial embarrassment had vanished into space and had been replaced by soft rhythmic caresses.

The little finger was a roguish rascal in comparison to the index finger, which assumed a martial air. It became evident that it was a matter of sparring fingers and that, in some way, during periods in which they were not together, they couldn't even stand one another. For a while the hand stroked every nook and cranny of the foot, on top of the silken weave. Then the fingers went into frantic action, while the toes contorted suggestively. The hand, guided by the ring finger, which had been the most active yet quiet of all, crept under the anklet to eliminate the foot's last vestige of resistance. The sun came out, and fingers and toes intertwined with tears under the nails. Then the blushing ceased. All defenses were down and the hand's roughness no longer existed.

With tightened grip and intermittent disentanglements the emotion of the moment raced unabated through the naked hand and foot. Fingers and toes intertwined, faintly caressing each other to the point of a scream, of a final scream.

Later, sounds began to filter in, things began to return to their geometric shape. In the hall the metallic sounds of doors were heard. The family was returning from the cold. Blinded by the streaming light, she clumsily began to dress her foot while he hid his hand in his deepest pocket. When the family entered the living room, the two became eternal accomplices.

miss green

Once upon a time there was a woman, a green woman, green from head to toe. She wasn't always green, but one day she started turning green. Now don't think for a minute that she was always green on the outside. But one day, she started turning green until finally she was green inside and also green on the outside. A terrible calamity for a woman who in years past wasn't green.

We'll begin talking here about those earlier years. The green woman lived in a region where green foliage was very abundant, but the greenness of the flora had nothing to do with the greenness of the woman. She had a lot of relatives, but there wasn't a drop of green in any of them. Her father, and above all her mother, had very large brown eyes. Brown eyes that were always vigilant of their daughter who one day would be green outside and green inside. Brown eyes when she went to the bathroom, brown eyes in her bedroom, brown eyes at school, brown eyes in the park and on walks, and brown eyes, especially, when the young lady explored beneath her white organdy panties. Eyes, eyes, brown eyes, and more brown eyes everywhere.

One afternoon, while she imagined brown eyes watching her, the young girl fell off her swing and scraped her knee. She looked at the wound, and mixed with tiny drops of blood, she saw the color green. She couldn't believe it. So, on purpose she scraped the other knee and once again, green. She cut her cheek, and green. She covered herself with scrapes and scratches, green, green, and nothing but green inside. Of course, once she returned home, brown eyes, green with rage. They spanked the bottom that covered more green.

More than becoming frightened, the green child became sad. And, years later, she became even sadder when she discovered the first green mole on one of her thighs. The mole began to grow until it was a mole the size of the entire girl. Many dermatologists struggled with all this green, and they all failed. The green came from somewhere else. She was to be green, and green she remained. Green she attended high school, green at the university, green she went to movies and restaurants, and green she cried her eyes out every night.

A week before graduation, she began to reflect: "The boys don't like me because they're afraid that my greenness will be catching. Besides, they say that our children could also turn out to be a very dirty green, or just green all over. They say hello to me from far off, shouting: 'See you, Miss Green,' and they make me cry the saddest green tears. But from now on I will wear sky blue sandals, even if it makes those brown eyes angry. And it won't matter to me if they call me Miss Green, because I'll wear the prettiest color on my feet."

And so, that very night, the green woman began taking walks, showing off her blue sandals that made the people who saw her think of the sea and crystal clear afternoons. While saying, "This is a very pretty color", although in somewhat poor taste and tending toward green, she never imagined what it meant to wear blue sandals, and her luck changed. When the green woman walked through the drabbest side streets, people began thinking of strange fish and of beautiful mermaids; a most unexpected imagining woke up these sleepy houses.

"Thank you, green woman," they shouted as she passed.

If the green woman went out for a walk at dawn, the insomniacs' heads filled with happy flutterings and the songs and flight of birds through the skies where calmness settled on the horizon. Soon, they would fall asleep, dreaming that a blue woman was running her fingers through their hair.

Soon the fame of this blue-green woman spread throughout the city and everyone wanted to escape their boredom, cure their insomnia, experience fantastic dreams, or travel to the very edge of the blue sky.

One afternoon, while the green woman rested at home, someone knocked on her door. She straightened her green hair and opened the door. Framed in the doorway was a man, a violet-colored man, violet from head to foot. They looked into each other's eyes. The green woman saw in him a bewitching dragon. The violet man saw a cascade of fish. The violet man walked toward the green woman and the green woman walked toward the violet man. All of a sudden, the violet dragon flew into the waterfall and began to splash about until he was swept away by the current of fish.

Then, they closed the door.

midday's unpretentious woman

This unpretentious woman at midday, besides wearing large orange barrettes in her hair, has the unlikely name of Violet. You can find Violet within the walls of her home, emerging from a tobacco-colored door, behind her blue eyes and a loose yellow dress, with that discreet flare she offers the innocent April wind. But her natural environment is found in the tree-lined streets beneath an eastern sun that warms and creates oblique shadows in the morning. And Violet gravitates toward the distant freshness of white cloth, crossing paths with the sincere lilac color and purples of the bougainvillea and the bristly, flowery hair of the jacaranda. Saying Violet, eucalyptus, azalea and privet is to speak of the same space that throws silent voices heavenward in varied tonalities, simple and playful.

Violet walks at her natural pace, her body moves like the

imperceptible growth of shade plants that one day surprise us with their fiery presence, neither gloomy nor pretentious. The same daring luminosity brightens Violet's cheeks; she also demonstrates the principle that explains the flames that settle upon large branches when winter has passed. Her chin-length amber hair, slightly curled under at the sides, bounces with the same rhythm as the flow of her dress. They form a counter-pendular symmetry, guiding Violet's undulating movement and the asymmetrical swinging of her arms, on which fine amber-colored hair glistens in the heat that descends to Earth and rises from the sidewalks. The woman walks with precision because her long legs stride confidently along a well-defined road, momentarily pausing to look at a succulent vine, or to allow the cars to cross her solitary path along the tree-lined avenue.

She continues her stroll, confident in her dull, gold-colored shoes, with rounded toes and medium high heels, pretty and discreet. They suggest the relationship between this woman and the sun, that noble relative who will accompany her through the long spring and summer, offering her subtle counsel about light and shadow, about warmth and passion, about simple flowers and flirtatious insects. Her feet wear the spirit of the sun, her dress and hair the points of flame, her lips a hint of red flame, in her gaze a room full of sunlight. Violet moves the lines of her legs, free beneath the flowing fabric, which ends where her thighs begin. Her skin has been taking on the subtle sepia tones of certain twilights in May that mature toward the sienna daybreaks of June and July. Meanwhile, the woman goes about covered with that sepia darkness, destined for whiteness and warmth.

She chooses a cobblestone street and carries the brightness of her body and dress into a slightly denser vegetation, among ancient buildings that have hidden within their stones the passing of hundreds of Aprils, and whose high walls have allowed the climbing vines to deposit their green from which sprout tiny white, blue, and red fish. You could say, without a doubt, that the woman has left her former world and has always lived beneath those eucalyptus and honey locusts that will never reach the extended arms of the sun. Down this narrow breech of yesteryear the smells mix in naked discourse, they circulate slowly and penetrate Violet's hair, they embrace her face and slip down her oval neckline; the fragrant words tell her stories of women as beautiful as she who have traveled through that same legend. Violet, without meaning to, responds with the language of her body's fragrance and returns tactile phrases that combine with the eternal smells of that midday.

The moment the woman turns into an even narrower alley, her absence becomes evident on the road that she has just left. But the new alley begins to glow and now it is difficult to distinguish between the light of the vegetation and Violet's glow, as they meet, recognize each other, understand each other, and become one. To mention fire, April, pepper trees, the place of the sun, is to say that Violet continues along the borders of passion permitting the noble dampness of the walls to touch her slightly full lips. That caress descends to her bare shoulders and from there to her arms and to her full breasts, her waist and hips, until it stops at her legs. Violet is grateful because the dampness represents the sad message of the pampered semi-darkness, like the first gestures of tenderness, of that other vegetation where there also exists the candor of aroma, color, form.

The woman changes her rhythm and becomes more active, as if in ecstasy, letting fly her tiny flowers. That's the way her movements are, decisive, irreversible, similar to the change from winter to spring. And Violet understands this in the throbbing of her flexible muscles, just as music and a sleeping woman understand each other, as a deer and the oak tree, burning coal and incense.

She comes to the end of the alley and stops in front of a small cedar door; she knocks softly, then the door opens automatically and Violet enters closing it behind her. In the faint shadows, a light-colored wooden staircase appears, as she climbs confidently she is accompanied by the distinct echoes of her footsteps. She enters a living room furnished with low pine furniture, objects of lustrous crystal, sprays of multicolored wheat occupying discreet spaces, cushions of flowered Hindu fabric, old bronze and pewter figurines, blue glass ashtrays; everything arranged upon a white carpet with cinnamon spots reminiscent of goat skins. The room is pleasant and the woman raises her arms, she slowly twirls, dancing to the silence and then stops by resting her arms on her thighs. She removes her shoes, her feet receive the carpet's caress; she walks around the small center table delighting in each step.

Now, she stands before a half-opened door leading to a bedroom, she draws near and notices a thicker darkness, expectantly she enters. Before the freshness of a lime green bed, the body and clothing of Violet are fire: the barrettes, her hair, her face, her shoulders, the fine hair on her arms, her dress, her legs, her bare feet. Midday's unpretentious woman makes a decision and lets her hair down completely. Shaking it slowly she creates shimmerings in the shadows. She approaches the bed, reaches for the bedspread, stroking it for a long time, then pulls it back, uncovering the sheets.

While Violet removes the flames that cover her and a raging fire lights up the bedroom, April enters the room naked. They stretch out on the white fabric, in the precision of the pampered semi-darkness, in the complicity of silence, and there begins another plasticity of aroma, color, form, exchanges of light and shadow, subtle flowers and flirtatious insects, where new dampnesses will be overpowering.

complicated woman of the afternoon*

for Neda and Enrique Anhalt

They made their habitual appointment for six in the afternoon, at the *Parnaso* in Coyoacán square. You know perfectly well that this woman is punctual, as precise as the gradual setting of the sun. For that reason you arrived ten minutes early, in search of peace. Furthermore, you like to see her arrive at places surrounded by evening shadows in her tight-fitting, dark brown or green corduroy pants, with her reddish hair, wavy and short. You like the way she raises her arm to greet you with a distant smile on her tan face and her rhythmic manner of walking between the tables. Then you stand and greet her with a kiss on the cheek, you invite her to take a seat, you help her with her chair, you whisper a little compliment about her brown low-heeled

*A phrase from Germán List Arzubide

shoes, as sober as the ochre light that strikes the walls of the San Juan Bautista church. You would like her to begin the conversation, since you know she is bubbling over with words, many and diverse words, funny descriptions, experiences that have nearly disappeared but find renewed energy in her memory. You also like to listen to her because of her firm voice, somewhere between sharp and gruff, her precise enunciation through those lips that clearly sculpt the sounds from within a thinly defined mouth.

When you met her at that party that ended at *El Riviere,* a night spot where the Combo San Juan was playing, you thought she was a delicate woman, from a *nouveau riche* family, which led you to believe that she was out of her natural environment. In time, you learned that your intuitions had been correct, but with the difference that this woman had studied physics and not law, as most of her family had done. During the following days as you chatted with her, you perceived a lurking anger in her, sharpened by the years, held in check through great effort, and you chose at that time not to awaken it. You showered her face with light caresses and a tenderness perfect as tiny daisies. You did not want those harsh, strong, irreversible words to come out against you. Just listening to her, seeing her careful gestures, the movement of her long fingers and sepia-colored eyes, or the way she drinks coffee, the way she smokes, and that's all. You wanted to channel her existential anger toward another time, toward a certain significant absence, or toward the lost years on that difficult trail that was now bringing them together. Instead, you wanted these cutting words to remain outside the limits of your afternoon meetings.

Under those circumstances, your conversations turned into a kind of delicate, ceremonial combat, which she just barely perceived, since you started the strategy of a truce without having engaged in any war. You knew that in a situation like that it was preferable to adopt the most subtle of ambiguities, choosing, on your part, to mix the yes and the no or to be prepared to change one to the other as soon as the woman's opinion seemed destined to shackle you. In that way you prolonged the time that you spent together, which always came to an end with the arrival of the first hint of darkness. You would say good-bye pleasantly and her words would accompany you.

Among your secrets is your inclination to watch women, to listen to them, to understand them in all their diverse manifestations, without having to live through love. About them you can remember only one way of dancing, one intense gaze that you discovered from inside at a moment of weakness, or one way of lifting a glass at those moments of intense female intimacy. Of course you have been able to show her this tendency, since you realize that she would become very resentful, given her twenty-five years of age. This complicated your relationship even more; you should have been a little more aloof and less interested in her: one moment be very interested and then make a cautious retreat, or skillfully direct the discussion to some other topic that could be too difficult for her. It was a matter of protecting the disguised fetishes that you knew were out-of-date, but not populist because you approach women that move you to feel light and measured joy, similar to the sunsets that cover a calm sea, or the pleasant thoughts that arise from clamorous, dispersed, saffron-colored light coming from a damp and lush vegetation.

The woman you were waiting for while drinking a cup of coffee, immersed in the tameness your jealously guarded laziness affords you, that woman with whom you shared this dense and filthy city, who had already transported you, by way of her sepia eyes like an aromatic river, to the pleasure of pristine landscapes that dozens of generations have enjoyed. Perhaps she had already discovered the voyages that you were taking in the humid gaze of that woman, and therefore, without intending to, she agreed to the careful and clean arrangement. The time her purple sweater, covered in front with tiny sienna-colored flowers, began to change into lavender up around her shoulders, or when the simple, old-gold comb, which held back the curls of her reddish hair, as if an ancient sun were shining through the foam that he himself was painting. Perhaps she had sensed the marvelous visions that she aroused in you. Maybe also for that reason, the one you began to call "complicated woman of the afternoon," started wearing faded jeans and a modest blouse as if to point you toward paths leading to terrible new urban landscapes. But you pretended not to understand. And you went into battle wielding your polished ambiguity, moving agilely in the face of contradictions, anger's obscure insinuations, the message which while spinning between careful strategies and trickery, covertly referred to you.

On those evenings you felt the need to confess your fetishes to her and to explain to her the blessings of relating to a woman through the strength of nature; explain that she specifically had awakened in you moments of clear understanding through her vivid stories, her hair, her eyes, her tiny nose, her thin lips, and her firm, medium-sized body. This had nothing to do with the lowly fixation of the burlesque, which you yourself detested. But you stopped when the confession was at the point of truly developing, because you were certain that the complexity of the situation would increase, in that you would find yourself obligated to begin a philosophical and ridiculous, poetic and childish discourse, and adding to that her perceptions, her methodical questions, her mathematical objections, her arguments of rebuttal. Then the battle would clearly tend to move into the territory of the "complicated woman of the afternoon."

These thoughts entered your mind between ten to six and six twenty at a table in the *Parnaso,* without your realizing that time was passing. As you looked at the clock and took into account the minutes that had passed, a certain nervousness modified your sense of laziness; because of the woman's well-known punctuality, you assumed there would be some delicate problems, monstrous setbacks, inevitable tragedies. You looked toward the church, the route she always took. Excited, you saw her appear on the sidewalk across from the *Parnaso*. Her hair was curlier than usual, a dark cherry-red blouse, loose-fitting, rested on her hips, and underneath a pair of *Edoardos* jeans accompanied by tennis shoes that were also cherry-colored. From that sidewalk she spotted you and waved her bare right arm; you saw the pleasant portrait created by a smile on her tan face, the usual smile.

At the instant she crossed the street you began to decipher the symbols that adorned her. Everything was the same as on other occasions, but today there was something new and alarming: twenty minutes late together with an artificial plainness and a wild hairdo. Maybe this would be the last battle.

behind the door

For Miriam, her day completes a cycle tonight. Perhaps it would be necessary to mention her face-cleansing lotion, her orange bath robe and the eyelids that she can hardly keep open. But Miriam simply considers these nocturnal rites as part of the fatigue of zero hour; a point at which she no longer wishes to know anything more about herself. León, a half-hour later, closes the door of his house behind him, and thinks in a very literary tone: I close the door behind me. For Miriam, the day is over. She adds: nevertheless, for me the darkness barely begins: that idea of not wanting to be alone with my body. León knows that he has no other recourse but to speak as though forced to write a story. In the darkness, in other words, in his loneliness, it is impossible to prolong the story. Today, and it may continue for a week, he held or has held Miriam in his arms, just as he might have held Connie or Mary, although he dislikes the name Mary. And of course he has said many times: hold them in my arms. For León the important thing is to hug them tightly, enjoy their breasts to the fullest, massage the white hips that passed, pass, and will pass through his hands. It is inevitable. But what difference can there be between Connie's hips and Miriam's hips or between Connie's breasts and Mary's breasts? A difference of atomic weight, diameters, areas; and this is where it all comes to a head. This is what causes León to disguise his own thoughts in literary phrases, and to construct a journalistic life for the small group of poets and literary people who surround him. Now, after closing the door, he would have preferred not to have gone to Switzerland with Miriam. Instead he might have picked up a two-bit female on Juanacatlán or Insurgentes Avenue, in order to immerse himself in the supply and demand of a cheap little world of monotonous caresses, to collect a debt that no woman owes, in order to demand the aberrations that Connie and Miriam postpone for another time. Until never. León calls this matter, the Darkness. And from where he stands he imagines Miriam seated at her dressing table. A Miriam who rubs her own breasts as if León continued to exist just there beyond her hands, but all of a sudden she stops the caressing remembering how demanding León was: the entire situation was inverted one hundred and eighty degrees, a difference of longitude and latitude. And he told her so, with all the cynicism of a journalist, just like a cartographer of New Spain.

"So that's what you wanted from me. Well, you barked up the wrong tree this time, buddy."

"No, it wasn't that. You don't understand that it has to do with another dimension, that after walking down the same street for a whole week it's necessary to take a short cut, down that alley that you were always afraid of before. It's a whole other dimension, honey."

"Shall we go?"

"No, it had nothing to do with that."

Miriam, by then, had already put on her pantyhose and her brassiere. León's streets and alleys. At other times he talked of avenues and thoroughfares, but the idea was the same: to take a short cut. His conversations never lacked a short cut. León couldn't write a story without enigmatic streets, despite the fact that none of his characters would ever walk down them. León insisted that literature without deserted streets was a literature that falsified the lives of its characters. And he was afraid that Romero might discover the different levels of discourse: the person in bed and the person of the literary club; because he knew that Romero would come out with it in some conference, in front of some other Miriam and the entire literary circle. Romero was likely to do that, you have to look out for yourself. But I'm careful about everyone. My day isn't over yet, I have to put up with myself for five more hours at night. And while León thinks about that damned Romero, about the night, about Miriam, about being careful about everyone, he retraces his steps and opens the door, and he cannot tell whether it's because of the light from the street lights or because of the alley he's looking for, but the darkness lifts, begins to dissipate. I retrace my steps and open the door.

yurécuaro

During the afternoon we had been playing split the top; Luis broke mine before we went in to eat. Even though I didn't show any emotion in front of Luis and Chicken, losing my top really hurt. It'd be just like wrecking your Formula I in a demolition derby; a person becomes fond of things that in the end are just toys. When you look at a box of marbles you're reminded of dusty pants, the clatter of marbles in the hand, and Mom's constant badgering, although it's Vicenta who goes up to the rooftop and comes down with the small tub of clothes, holding it with one arm, as if she held a bundle of clothes by the river in Yurécuaro. And it's true, because when she climbs the spiral stairs, besides showing off her brown thighs, the color of a varnished closet, her hair bounces against the sky and air and against the roar of a fleeting Jumbo Jet. Then I think of Yurécuaro and Vicenta walking through the almond grove against the gurgling of the river and the singing of the birds coming from the tragacanth bushes;

that's where the smell of her hair mixes with spearmint.

Before eating I put away the pieces of my top, and I heard my mother say:

"I'm warning you, Alex, the next time it happens I'll let you go hungry. Vicenta went and called you four times and your royal highness kept on rolling around in the dirt as if you hadn't heard a thing."

"I couldn't come, Mom. Until the game was over, I couldn't; because, then, Luis and Chicken start saying things about you. You wouldn't want them to say dirty things to me about you, would you?"

"I'm just telling you, I don't care about those little bums."

And during the entire meal, between going back and forth for the tortillas, halfway between the meatballs in red chili sauce, Mom insisted that our house was not a hotel, that the other night was my third (and final) abuse of the right to stay out late, that during the day I'm still a baby who has to be changed and that at night I want to act like a man, that she didn't go through all this to be someone's servant, and Vicenta comes and goes from the kitchen to the dining room with a smirk on her face and you don't know whether it's out of irony or stupidity. The steam from the soup hides her face, but from both sides of the white columns of steam bounce Vicenta's tits and my mom with hurry up and finish so you can go cash the money order, and from the stairs she adds:

"Don't act like you're deaf."

Then Vicenta asks me if I saw the girls' bus go by, that she saw it go by when she was at the tortilla store, because for sure Rosa, the girl from the house on the corner, was on it. I tell her yes, that I saw it out of the corner of my eye, that Rosa wasn't sitting in the window seat because she's been mad since yesterday.

"Personal things, Vicenta."

Before arriving at the telegraph office, I parked my Formula I at the house on the corner, and, Rosa don't be like that, it wasn't my fault, I'll come by for you around seven, later we'll talk about the thousands of things that you want to tell me, don't be like that. O.K. While I started my engine (I really like the sound of these pipes), I thought that I'd better cash the money order from my dad because that way I'd make my 1% right off, before my mom takes out the 1/2%. This week you don't deserve it. But, what can I do with only 1/2% when my expenses keep going up: Rosa's worth something, a cone, a pop or at least some chocolates like the ones in the shape of a rabbit.

That business about the top shouldn't bother me, since I'm already a man of thirteen going on fourteen, but even as old as I am, I hate having my top split in two like a pear. Luis was really happy about it and Chicken, serves you right, prrr, nah nah nah nah *nah* nah, so your Morelia top was so great, huh?, serves you right, prrrrrr, the ones down at the market are better, and all Luis had to do was smile. Chicken has always been like that, he's a twitchy little girl. Of course at his age he ought to cut out those nah nah nah nah *nah* nahs, Chicken uses most of the put-downs that a little nine-year-old girl would use on you. But because Luis defends him, I didn't dare kick the shit out of him; besides, I had lost and if I showed them I was mad, Chicken would start in again with his prrrs and nah nah nah nah *nah* nahs.

"Do you have any identification?"

"My mom's social security card."

"How much are you cashing, young man?"

"The money's in my pants," I shouted to Mom from the shower. The 1% was hidden in my shorts, just in case, because you can expect anything from Mom. Even though I would have preferred to take a spit bath, Vicenta, your bath is ready, Mrs. Eugenia told me to turn on the boiler for the filthy little bum; I got to figuring how long it would take you to get here and for your bath to be ready, and since you always go at a turtle's pace, while coming along Heliópolis street, you'd stop to watch the kids from Irapuato play, then coming down Nilo you'd turn on Nubia and go to the house on the corner, so you could stand around watching to see if maybe Rosa would come out. And when you'd come through the kitchen door your bath would be waiting for you nice and hot, I even got out your clothes.

"You're wrong, I came in my Formula I."

"But don't tell me you didn't stop your car to watch the boys on Irapuato street?"

"You're wrong, I don't like watching those bums play, they're just a bunch of dummies."

Vicenta mixes everything up, she talks and talks without thinking, and if something suddenly occurs to her, she'll tell you that, and then go on with what she was saying, but she can come up with thousands of crazy, mixed-up stories and then later on she decides on the real one, it's like what my math teacher says, that from a false premise you can come up with the right answer, because that's the way math is. No one understands what the word "answer" means, but I'll bet the kids can imagine all kinds of strange four-footed beasts; as far as I'm concerned, I believe that the correct answers that come from false premises have got to be some pretty scary animals, like the ones that chase me in that dream I always have. That's got to be what's going on in Vicenta's mind, her head must be crammed full of bugs from the sticks. When I think about her, what I see are country scenes, she sees bugs from the country and from nowhere else. If she's carrying a bucket I see a clay pot dripping wet, and if her hair is down I fix it up in a certain way so that I see her walking through the house with freshly woven braids and then the wall disappears and behind it I can see almond trees where Vicenta walks. And when she's about to cross the river, if she's got on petticoats down to her ankles, I imagine her body in such a way that when she's crossed the river she walks barefoot on the stones, and her petticoats have disappeared and Vicenta is a body the color of the varnish on the closet, and I'm in the grass, leaning against a eucalyptus tree, waiting for her. Now I see her in front of me with her little tits just like at night in my room and we do those little things that she taught me and that a few days ago I taught Rosa, Rosey. But I don't understand the words Vicenta whispers when she gives me those little bites, she says them in a dialect that is only understood in Yurécuaro. And I think that she's mad at me because of Rosa, and she gets my bath ready on time, on purpose, even though she knows without a doubt that I prefer washing myself because I'm always in a hurry, because Vicenta imagines with her country-bug mind that Rosey, Rosa and I do the things that she taught me.

"I'll bet you're going with Rosa to the vacant house."

It's possible that she's been spying on us, but maybe she's imagining that we go inside the Marquina's house. I've never noticed anyone spying on us, much less Vicenta, because we're always careful. Even if there are swallows on the power lines we don't go in, we'd rather cool it.

I finished bathing and left like a shot for Rosa's house. In Don Chuy's store, Luis and Chicken were drinking a soda, and Chicken made fun of my bad luck and my top from Morelia again. Then I couldn't stand it any longer and, though Luis always defends him, I called him a sonofabitch. And a little farther down the street, just in case, almost in front of the Marquina's house, I said: damn Chicken, you've got an ass like Cuqui the Rat.

"When God made you he made a mistake, 'cause he made you good, but only from the waist down."

"Just wait, shithead," was the only thing Luis said.

Chicken is in charge of choosing friends, and Luis says nothing about it, except in the case of Guty, who owns some really juicy things:

1. A bike with Alce Blanco-type handlebars
2. An Anáhuac poster
3. A Kryptonite stone (that Chicken didn't dare look at)
4. A mom who gives them nut cookies and jamaica punch
5. A soccer ball.

But at times no one comes out of Guty's house for days, and no one knows if people are mad at them or if they just get bored with all the treasures that surround them. On afternoons when they don't have any friends to attack, they hang around leaning up against the Pepsi-Cola machine until Don Chuy closes.

While slowing down by throwing it into second from third, I thought that Luis wouldn't do anything to me because he enjoys it when, from time to time, people make fun of Chicken; besides, Luis feels like he's at a disadvantage around me, the same as other guys on the block; the reason: Rosa, Rosey. Of course some of them have girlfriends, like Guty, who, by using all his toys, made one of the best conquests of all, but they don't trust him or me and a few others either, because you can see the envy in their faces when they see us go by with our hair parted just right and with our shoes shined up pretty good. I parked my Formula I across the street from the house on the corner, I let the engine cool down, two or three pumps on the throttle and carefully turned the key off. Rosa was waiting for me sitting in the chair her mom uses for knitting in the afternoon, near the climbing vines in the garden. It was one of those smoggy evenings, everything got fuzzy but you could see Rosa because of the brightness of the last few rays of light. The smog felt like grains of sand rubbing around under our eyelids. Right when Rosa said: I've been waiting for you for a long time, my mom could get after me again, Vicenta appeared in the darkness of the vines and in the slight glint of Rosa's eyes. Things were getting fuzzy and among the vines I could almost believe that I was seeing the outline of Vicenta approaching the eucalyptus tree that I was leaning against, I smelled the scent of her hair mixed with the smell of spearmint, and it was Rosa taking me by the arm and her hair, being so close, took on the name of Rosa's hair, so Vicenta would remain suspended, quiet, with her arms reaching out to an Alex who also remained suspended, paralyzed between the tragacanth bush and Vicenta's body.

"If you want to, we can take a walk down Clavería avenue and then we'll go . . ."

"First, I'd like to know why you called me a scaredycat little girl; well, do you think you're such a big man? You were playing with tops, you're not so hot."

"Only while we waited for the bus. Besides, you weren't sitting by the window. You're not so hot yourself."

"Don't change the subject on me, scaredycat."

"Let's not fight again, forgive me and I'll forgive you, O.K.?"

We left the car parked so we could walk over to Clavería avenue, it's always good to stretch your legs a little. In China Park we hid in the trunk of an ahuehuete tree, just like other couples. I like the darkness of the park because no one messes with anyone there and you never know if the ones in the tree next to you might be your cousin and the Buchán's maid, or a couple of real lovebirds. Rosa's tits are a little bit bigger than Vicenta's although Vicenta is bigger than Rosa, and because Rosa is fat she should have tits like freshly peeled grapefruits. Vicenta kisses me like a toilet plunger and Rosa's kisses are as sweet as lollipops. Vicenta's legs are the best even though Rosa's are fleshier and Vicenta's hands are like cedar and Rosa's like organdy. We left the ahuehuete tree behind along with the whispering of the other couples. We hardly ever say anything before arriving at the Marquina's house, we think that by staying quiet we won't be seen by the prying eyes of the people who come and go from Don Chuy's store.

We run in like a shot, the iron gate no longer squeaks because the other day I came and oiled it because of a suggestion my mom made without knowing what she was saying: a cautious woman is worth her weight in gold, I always have three liters of oil on hand, just in case.

So you oil because of busybodies and a squeaky gate, and the fear of getting in is now resolved. We have to go around on the walkway by the patio to get into the house through the dining room door, the sound of our shoes on the ground that once had been good grass made us shiver a little, but we weren't as scared once we made it to the kitchen and even less when we climbed the stairs, but now it isn't fear but terror that grips Rosa who screams out in the darkness of the Marquina's house, and my own terror because I hear sounds coming down the staircase, and Rosa who continues to scream while she stands in the middle of the stairs and who also hears the sounds that turn into a pair of silhouettes blending together like tree branches while coming at us and everything turns into laughter, side-splitting laughter at the sight of Chicken trying to pull up his pants, muttering something like you'd better not make fun of me. And Rosa doesn't know whether to laugh or to be scared when Luis says to me: If you rat on us, I'll bust your face. I fall down on the dirty floor, my sides splitting, laughing, while the sounds fade in the distance. I begin to calm down, my breathing comes back to normal, now I can hear clearly the thumping of my heart in my ears and feel Vicenta's hands rub my stomach, the sound of Yurécuaro's river blends with the murmur of the eucalyptus trees and Vicenta's dark hair covers my eyes and all I can smell is mint.

anything goes

They'll never be able to take from him that air of being a magician. He tries to be convincing by emphasizing the most insignificant information, and then surprise his listener with some other detail in which the important element appears. It's as if Neftalí knows intuitively that no one will believe him when he waves his arms among nonexistent handkerchiefs and rabbits. During the Elvis years, his favorite was Pat Boone, the opposite of the King of Rock'n'Roll. Of course in those days no one paid any attention to how serious he was about being a magician. A possible explanation for his penchant for exaggerated explanations might be that Neftalí was a newcomer to the club, to the school, and really to any place the middle-class kids go to see and be seen. He wore short pants well into the sixth grade, and we teased him for looking like a sissy, that the time for lollypops and a little beanie hat was long gone. When the bus would drop him at his house we would yell all kinds of crude things at him. Even the kids in fourth grade dared to call him names. He must have put up a real fight to force his mother to let him wear long pants and the brown and yellow checkered shirts that we all liked so much because they made us look like rich American kids. Around the middle of the year, things started to get out of hand. New insults started flying around the room, but in a few days he was back to being the same old Neftalí. The English Cockatoo defended him tooth and nail just to look good to the Dubers, that is, to Mrs. Nelia Duber, who chatters more than a family of parrots in a tree. His mother, Nené, really goes to extremes. She takes any fad to ridiculous lengths, probably because she made a career out of showing off to her lady friends in the area. Now I understand what Neftalí was up to with his old tricks: he would tell us that his father would give him thousands of pairs of pants, but by the next morning they all had been cut off short, and that of course the pants thief wasn't a rat or anything like that, it was the sewing lady who would steal the legs of his pants to patch the knees of her own kids' pants. Then someone would say to him: you're still a crybaby, your mother still powders your bottom.

I don't know why I began to think about Neftalí, but the two sets of tennis that I just beat him at, and his racquet flying over the net and over my head brought back that other defeat, during the field trip at the end of our freshman year of high school. My going on to sophomore was guaranteed because of my good grades and the scholarship they gave me. To a certain extent, I was also an outsider in the midst of all those blond-headed kids, in that school of endless, highly polished hallways. Neftalí would rather have stayed at home listening to his Pat Boone collection, thinking about some Julieta he was inventing bit by bit, or about his roles as the Great Houdini in the bathroom or under the sheets. That was the last time I saw him on a school field trip. Those gigantic picnics were by far the most coveted, because the top ten in each grade were awarded a trip to San Miguel Regla. It was good politics, because one way or another the parents received something from the school besides complaints and the regular bill. So the little geniuses went on their spiritual weekend. Many of us already knew the place, but now it wasn't the same as when we were accompanied by our families.

I said before that it was a defeat, but to tell you the truth I wouldn't know what to call it. Sometimes you just classify something that happens without really thinking about it. It could have been a defeat, it might not have been, who knows? Friday night I called him on the phone and I guess both of us were nervous because neither of us could sleep. He insisted on taking the football helmet that Nené, his mother, had given him, and also a pool cue like Joe Chamaco used to use. The toys that Nené had heaped up in Neftalí's bedroom had him believing that his arrival in this world was her entire justification for living. I convinced him not to take along so many things because San Miguel Regla had pool tables with cues and everything, ping-pong tables, and no one would want to play touch football with a pool there and horses and thousands of trees all around the ranch. In the end he took along some badminton racquets that he never used. I wouldn't say that Neftalí was the only bullheaded one, of course. Most of us took a million things that stayed locked up, together with the desire to destroy them.

Right now he's probably in the sauna, trying to get over being mad. It won't be long before he arrives squeezing an accordion of words and apologies between his hands, trying to get back on my good side. He will offer to buy me another cognac and I'll accept just so he'll stop waving his arms around, and I'll say: It's O.K., Neftalí, don't worry about it, we know each other. Then I'd like to add that I remember our high school years, and particularly the field trip to San Miguel Regla, and I'd like to hear your opinion, Neftalí, so we can have a good laugh or perhaps cry a little, and maybe we can finish off the bottle of Martell, smoking while we play a match, and remind you of your ridiculous bag with the racquet handles sticking out on all sides. Neftalí, do you remember? Shit, man, those were the days. I like to remember those things, because that morning it had rained and, from the window, the vegetation outside seemed to be asleep. The buses were splashing through the puddles as if they were water tortillas left in the road by some Indian woman from Pachuca. And the boys, all of us, hiding behind our rosy cheeks, not giving a damn about the 201st squadron and the Korean War, despite its having ended several years before. In Mexico they continued to praise that glorious squadron. After the winding curves announced by the signs, after going through such towns as Real del Monte, Chico and Huasca, we arrived at the ranch. Maybe at that moment Neftalí began to struggle against the tempests of adversity, because in the parking lot we found the Williams School's buses, and of course the girls from Williams, and especially that Julieta from the Williams School who both Neftalí and Urrieta were crazy about. Well, anyway, we scrambled off with all our junk, barely holding back our desire to shout obscene greetings to the Williams crowd. Mr. Soreli—Sister Soreli to us—began dividing us up into groups of five to a cabin. Neftalí and I stayed in El Mirador cabin, a few were lucky enough to stay in the Conde de Regla, or in the Condesa de Juana de Regla cabins. The caretaker who had the assignment of telling the stories about the people of the area recited the legend behind each cabin. In El Mirador cabin there had lived a baron who spent his time studying the pepper trees and describing the patterns formed by moss. Then he would draw his sculpted thoughts on special sheets of paper brought from Spain, or maybe from France. One of the baron's drawings is still displayed in the cabin, and while it looks like a ghostly image, the moss and the pepper trees and the freshness of the area do not appear anywhere in the crazy man's brush strokes.

That afternoon a few foolish boys went to swim in the pool's icy water. Some of us went on horseback as far as the lake to see a meaningless lighthouse in the middle of a lily-choked body of water. The guys with bad habits went to play dominoes. The ones with worse habits went to smoke under the pine trees or in the bushes. A simpler idea was to go for a long ride on horseback and stretch out on the daisies to smoke. Great big puffs that would mix with the cold mist while we looked up at the clear blue Chinese silk print, or maybe it was Japanese, or Oriental as our World History teacher would say in the event that we were unable to ascertain their exact nationality. That was simpler because on our return we met four beautiful horses ridden by an equal number of young women, and we saw ourselves as knights and all that stuff about Amadís, and hi! how ya doin', what a surprise, how are you Julieta, Princess Julieta as Neftalí wished he could have said. We're just out taking a little ride. We'll see you tonight at the campfire, bye Julieta, bye Princess Julieta as Neftalí wished he could have said.

Those experiences come back to me as if seen through blue carbon paper; blurred horses moving into the stable, and even more blurred is each of our futures: the predictable though sudden death of Ricardo Rodríguez, Neftalí's questionable success in the College of Engineering, my terrible indecision between creative writing and economics. That evening everything was about to be discovered, the useless homage to life would be revealed. Like now: I don't know if Neftalí will show up with his kaleidoscope of excuses—while that guy saws Eternal Beauty in two—just to tell me: It's my nerves, I'm having problems at the factory, lately I've been kind of sick, the workers are up to something, I'm fighting with Betty, she found out about you know who, people putting bugs in her ear, I went to see the doctor and he told me the same damn thing as always. He'll finish sawing her stomach in half, a few smiles, applause, boos, and although I would like to have Neftalí help me tear through that carbon paper, I'll say: forget it, man, let's not get into that. But he hasn't come and I'm nursing my third cognac and the silhouettes of the horses are barely visible. Before we entered the stable the sunlight was still filtering through the needles of the pines. When we came out, the lights had gone off like in a city blackout, those blackouts that show us walls and flowerpots in the middle of the hallway. But in San Miguel Regla we heard the sounds of nature, the rustling of the foliage brought to our imagination the incredible approach of some plant deity. In the cabins there was always hot water: everything available to soothe our bodies and feet. We went to the bonfire in danger of catching cold from our wet hair. When we walked up to the fire another cloud came over Neftalí's smiling face. They had something up their sleeve, and they didn't wait an instant to begin kicking Neftalí: Sister Soreli took Neftalí by the arm, in front of the girls and guys, above all the girls, and shouted in his ear: pervert. He dragged him off to El Mirador cabin, the people stopped dancing, and through the curtain of smoke and sparks from the bonfire, the whispers reached our ears. The versions of the message varied according to the size of the ears, and just like in the game "pass it on," by the time they got to my ears I couldn't tell whether they were true or exaggerated. But just like when the game is over, and the original words are revealed, I soon found out the real message.

Julieta:
When I see you pass by
I see you walking naked like a movie star.
When your back is turned to me
I just love your wonderful Marilyn Monroe hips.
When you are lying down

I dream of having you between my legs
just like in a Hollywood movie.
If you want to take a little walk
after the bonfire
I'll wait for you down by the river
where the little bridge crosses.
I'll have two horses there
so we can go fornicate in Uncle Tom's Cabin.
Neftalí Duber

I've reconstructed this message-poem poorly; a few words are missing while others are taking the place of key words. The verses at the beginning are interchangeable. Where I said *so we can go fornicate in Uncle Tom's Cabin* there ought to be some other cinematographic image, but I think that today the author would choose this one. If I repeated it I don't think it would come out the same; besides, every version loses the freshness of tone, the malicious intensity in which the original was written. When Julieta received the note she was furious and said: well, I didn't even like him, anyway. But she went immediately to His Grace, Sister Soreli, and reported the flagrant offense of "that dirty-minded kid." His Grace decreed that Neftalí should be left out of all recreational activities: You will remain inside El Mirador cabin until we return to Mexico City, and you'll be singled out as vermin non grata before the entire school. The guys couldn't have been more pleased. The general opinion was that a little excitement was necessary to give the field trip some sort of meaning. They weren't interested in the decision of the Council, nor did they think that Neftalí was vermin non grata. Most of us were already used to the Nostradamus Soreli's judgements. Anyway, everyone divided up into two groups because of that dirty trick by Urrieta, The Movie Freak. Now I call him a movie freak, but at that time I only knew that he really liked Jayne Mansfield and John Ford's horse operas. Both groups knew that Urrieta was responsible for the message-poem, and that he liked Julieta too, and that he was capable, in all his cynicism, of causing San Miguel Regla's wrath to fall upon Neftalí; and the two groups thought that no one should accuse Urrieta, that the situation should be resolved between Neftalí Duber and Marco Antonio Urrieta.

In the cabin Neftalí didn't say a word. The smoke from the chimney and the cigarettes made the air in El Mirador a little stuffy.

Neftalí was lying down, his gaze fixed on the beams in the ceiling, then his eyes followed the flight of a moth. All of us followed the sweeping flight of the insect around the lamp. Someone said: at 12:30 out by the lake. The badminton racquet handles were sticking out of the closet. It seemed as though Neftalí, rather than crying, had been thinking about the night, the river, Pat Boone, the pines, the figures in the flames, his fingers, The Crazy Baron, the years to come, The Great Houdini, the pepper trees, the lighthouse among the wild lily pads, and also about the gossip. We went out to eat. Neftalí remained lying there until we returned, and the moth was still flying around, stubbornly, as if searching for a tiny door in the lamp shade. The same voice said: Urrieta accepts. The only change in the cabin was the fireplace: the flames had gone out and only the coals were left crackling like red hot aluminum. There was nothing but silence until 12:25, now broken by our footsteps on the ashes. Then Neftalí stopped thinking and got up. We left the cabin. The moth also left.

Our group gathered around what had been a large bonfire. We poked at the coals that Urrieta's group had left, and each person raised a burning stick like a torch. I could make out the faces of Reséndiz, Sepúlveda, Castillo and I think Arce's; I could only sense the others there in the darkness. We walked toward the bridge. As we crossed it we saw the reflection of the torches in the river. They looked like flames drowning in the current. Neftalí had to walk in front of the two columns of boys. Torchless, he led the burning snake. We went up the hill. The night was full, overwhelming us, extending out to the lake, to the hills beyond, dwarfed by the torches, casting the forest's nocturnal animals into darkness. Don't burn my hair and I didn't know, sorry, were phrases that filled the air along with the fragrance of unclassifiable vegetation. They started to go down and, at about the middle of the slope, we could see the lighthouse and the fireflies that illuminated Urrieta's band, or the Invincible Legion, as the movie freak would put it. The double column picked up the pace, the rhythm of breathing accelerated and the fire snake began to gasp. The torches up ahead ceased to be fireflies, the silhouettes became masses of flesh and bone—At this instant in the torch of memory the blue carbon paper burned up—a shape without a jacket and without a torch pointed to the place where John Wayne Urrieta stood.

A different voice said: until one of the two says I give up. The first voice added: no help from anybody. We all formed a circle, Neftalí took off his jacket and rubbed his arms, while Urrieta pounded the palm of his left hand with the knuckles of his right. The fight began with the classic movements of feeling each other out, right jabs by each to make the other guy feint. Neftalí backs up, retreating, stumbles, Urrieta jumps like a panther on the fallen body, a murmur goes up from the crowd that is muffled by the first groans from the flurry of arms and legs, the bundle turns over and Neftalí is on top, he sits on Urrieta's stomach, he pounds him in the face and says damn you, Urrieta doesn't return the insult or the punches, his arms are pinned under Neftalí's legs, a blotch near his nose tells us that Urrieta is bleeding, no one knows where his strength comes from, but Neftalí rolls over to one side, more murmurs, some of the torches have gone out, they're standing again, Urrieta, determined, throws a right cross and then several hooks to the body, Neftalí withstands the attack and they clinch, they break and Urrieta, insulting Neftalí's mother while wiping the blood with his forearm, suddenly kicks Neftalí in the stomach, a few voices say: that's not fair. Others answer: anything goes; now only a few torches remain lit, Neftalí moves backwards, the circle breaks, and the scuffling on the ground begins again, both fighters throw a lot of wild punches, they are like an Aztec goddess with all those arms, they roll down the slope until they stop at the edge of the lake, with the faint light that remains we are able to distinguish Urrieta's arm as it picks up a rock and strikes Neftalí on the forehead, now they are both bleeding from the face, turning, they fall into the water and this time Neftalí takes a rock and smashes it against John Wayne Urrieta's head, the mumbling of the crowd increases when the last torches go out, the night reappears and we hear the splashing of two bodies in the water, a voice says: stop the fight and other shouting voices agree, the night seems black as pitch, the lake becomes a silent pool and Neftalí calls out my name and who knows what else, while Urrieta's group searches for a body in the water.

gertrudis

for Marco Antonio Campos

Tonight, when I returned to my little room, I began to cry and after calming down a little I'm still sad. I felt like writing this letter to nobody in particular, since I don't believe anyone could be interested in my story. And I'm saying this, not because I'm old, skinny, lacking a few teeth, and have always been sort of ugly, but because my jobs have never been interesting nor has my social condition ever changed in my entire life. As a young man I started out as a traveling salesman peddling turtle eggs downtown at the corner of Palma and Tacuba, and, from time to time, at night, at certain establishments that rent rooms by the hour. Later, I sold poor quality flat irons in the vicinity of Clavería and Azcapotzalco.

I sold eggs, supplies for *Del Fuerte*, and maids' clothing door to door. And I always went from pushing one thing to pushing another without success, without ever being able to put aside any savings. I was single until I was forty-three; I could barely support myself.

A few minor doorway or cheap hotel love affairs, but never anything lasting. When loneliness really began to eat away at me, I came across Gertrudis.

Today, I tend a small newspaper stand in the Doctores district, an area that has really gone to the dogs, but I no longer have any desire to continue with the business. In Nezahualcóyotl City it always seems to be evening and it's all the same to me. It doesn't even matter to me whether it's day or night or if I arrive late to pick up the newspapers. And if that wasn't enough, last Thursday a pickup truck crashed into the corner where I have my stand, left it all twisted up. For a long time now I've been thinking that the only thing missing would be for a pigeon from the cathedral to shit all over me. If my sales had dropped off before the accident, now with all that twisted metal people won't even come near. They pass right by without stopping, headed for Vértiz or, if not there, toward Cuauhtémoc, to one of those big stands where they have a larger variety of magazines, books and newspapers.

I have to admit that there was a moment in my life when I improved my economic situation. There was a man—later I found out that he was a lawyer—a young man and a real talker who always had a joke on the tip of his tongue, kind of bald and thin like me, who always bought *La Prensa* and pin-up magazines from me. It was obvious that he either liked me or felt sorry for me, but the important thing was that he called me Don Chucho and not just Chucho, like the people from Doctores do. Well, this man asked me, while he thumbed through *Caballero* magazine, if I wouldn't like to work for him as a messenger in his office. I immediately said yes. A few days later I took my stand home and told my old lady I was going to work in an office. Gertrudis liked the idea. I was going to make a lot of cash that we could use to go to Villa del Carbón or to Oaxtepec on the weekends. Besides, Gertrudis liked to fix herself up and look sexy.

I started living with this gal when I was already along in years. Gertrudis had become a widow five years earlier and had been sleeping around without any special man. Her two sons lived in the United States; at first, they sent her a few dollars, but later she lost track of them. She was sure that they had been killed, but I'll bet that they're still up there running around, living high on the hog, never worrying about their mother. At any rate, my old lady and I kept each other company and helped each other out. She set up a little table outside the neighborhood where she sold tiny bottles of sugar, candies, chocolates, *Kangaroo* gum, and other sweets that the kids from the area bought from her. When I got my first bimonthly checks, and we could say that we had a little extra money, we expanded the business and she began selling *Larín* chocolate bars, honey bars and coconut candy, goats-milk candy wafers, Japanese peanuts, even cigarettes, pear candy covered in chili powder, and wrestler-mask candies. With these earnings, Gertrudis began to stash away a little money on the side, and she really seemed to be happy.

At the office, the fact was that I very seldom worked as a messenger. Furthermore, I didn't wear a uniform but simply pants and a fairly nice jacket, always the same. And when I'd get home, I'd take them off and slip into my old overalls. Well, at the office the lawyer who recommended me, whose name was De la Torre, as talkative inside as he was on the street, introduced me to the personnel as an errand boy, or something like that: "Don Chucho," he said, "is here to serve you, if you want cigarettes, a soda or coffee, whatever, he'll bring it to you." They also had me dust off the desks, empty the garbage, package magazines, and attach labels with white *Resistol* glue.

The problem was that I had to label about two thousand five hundred envelopes a week, not counting the errands and the cleaning and a thousand little favors. Well, even though I was making more money, I started feeling pretty bad since there was a world of difference between having my own business and working as everyone's slave. Especially at my age, when I had always been independent.

Little by little I was getting madder and madder and I really became angry when I'd hear, Don Chucho, bring me some *Raleighs,* some *Marlboros*, and go send this telegram, the magazines have arrived. Even though sometimes I'd give them a dirty look or act like I didn't understand, I put up with it because I saw that Gertrudis was really happy. And she'd say to me, don't worry about it, don't pay any attention to them. Then, De la Torre told me that when there was a lot of work I'd have to stay late. The problem was that there was always more and more work. I would return to the neighborhood late at night, without having been able to let Gertrudis know; and she'd let me in with funny looks and an irritated attitude. One time I even had to stay all night at the office because I had to prepare some very important documents. My old lady didn't like that at all. She started hounding me unfairly, she'd be mad and start saying things like: Jesus, don't come in so late. Jesus, who do you think you are. Jesus, do I look like an idiot. And I: Woman, it's not my fault. Woman, it's for our own good. Woman, go talk to De la Torre. I was between a rock and a hard place and my anger grew to the point of desperation.

The time came when Gertrudis no longer said anything. She was silent and withdrawn. At night she'd be snoring when I came in, as if I didn't mean a damn thing to her. The truth is that I liked her screaming and threats better than a quiet, hostile woman who would throw a bowl of soup in front of me, wouldn't make my refried beans and would leave a pile of dishes in the sink. With the earnings from her business, she bought nice clothes, while I never had a suit that would help me be promoted to messenger. But I liked the idea of her wearing nice shawls.

Pretty soon, she started putting on so much makeup it made her look like a clown; sometimes I wouldn't even find her at home when I got off work early. Just like when I first met her, she started drinking. One day, drunk to the gills and cursing everyone in the neighborhood, she really let me have it on the patio of the apartment complex. Then, one night she never came home and I never saw her again.

Not long after that, the neighbor ladies told me that Gertrudis had been running around with the guy with the sweet potato cart, a fat old guy with a Pancho Villa mustache. They said that when he would come by stirring up the dust with his steam-engine whistle, he would stop in front of the candy stand as the sun was setting and talk to my old lady without giving a second thought to his sweet potatoes. Afterwards he stopped coming by, but instead my woman would close up the business early and would take off all dolled up and everything, and that she would return mussed up and with her hair down. They suddenly told me all this. I didn't want to hear any more.

I didn't even try to look for Gertrudis. It was clear that, although she was getting on in years, she liked to fool around. She had made her bed and now she would have to sleep in it. After that incident, madder than ever, I resigned from my job at the office without saying thanks to anyone. I moved out of the area and took a room in Nezahualcóyotl City and put my newsstand up again in the Doctores district.

A while back, when I was riding in a bus at night, at one of the stops I heard the steam-engine whistle that sweet potato venders use. All of a sudden all the sadness that I had never felt before, or that I had been hiding somewhere, hit me. I went into my room and began to cry uncontrollably; later, I wrote these pages that won't interest anyone. And I feel that this sadness will never leave me, and that instead it is getting deeper and deeper. I believe that I am about to die. I can't find any other explanation.

outside the ring

Rodolfo went into the bar. He didn't ask for anyone, he simply remained standing in front of the bar. In the opposite corner, at the next to the last table, there were two men: his manager and a younger man. Rodolfo asked for a beer, paid for it immediately and, while gulping it down without pausing, a few drops stained his cherry-colored tie. He searched for his face in the mirror, his left eye began to twitch when he couldn't find a trace of his features. The only thing reflected was the labelless backs of the bottles on the bar. He wiped his mouth with his forearm and this time stained the sleeve of his white suit. His manager greeted him by raising his glass, the young man smiled pleasantly at him. The boxer did not respond to the greeting of either, he remained standing in front of the bar, he bent one leg to rest it on the rail. After drinking another beer he insisted on finding his face, the twitch became more pronounced when he observed that the nape of the bartender's neck was really there in the mirror. He raised his arm as if to pull his shirt out of his coat and realized that not even his arm appeared in the mirror.

At his table, the young man mixed a Castillo rum and Coke for himself. He nibbled on some peanuts.

"It looks like Rodolfo already read the reviews in *Ultimas,*" pointing at the newspaper under the manager's elbow.

"He looks like a crazy man who's just lost it," said the manager.

"He didn't even say hello, he must really be pissed off," the young man added.

"It doesn't surprise me. Let's see if I can handle him," said the manager.

Rodolfo walked up to their table, and scratching his ear with his little finger, he said, "You're some kinda coward."

The manager tried to say something.

"Stay cool, Bro," interrupted the young man. "What's goin' on?"

"You know the newspapers never tell the truth," the manager said trying to clear himself.

"You're some kinda coward," Rodolfo insisted, wishing to add an appropriate expletive, but the words got stuck in his throat.

"So I come from the sticks, huh?" the boxer added.

Silence fell over the bar, the sound of a noisy muffler and the music from an organ grinder filtered in from Guerrero Avenue. The boxer grabbed the manager's lapels, shook him four or five times and let him go. The manager fell back underneath the last table. The young man attempted to stop Rodolfo, but the boxer, with a smashing blow, knocked him against the wall.

"So you didn't know anything about anything, huh?"

"Rodolfo," the young man shouted, as he saw Rodolfo pulling brass knuckles out of the inside pocket of his coat.

The manager was trying to stand up when the boxer threw the first punch, knocking him down again and a blood stain appeared beneath his ear. With that all-too-well-known mannerism of his, Rodolfo lifted his fist to the level of his cheeks. As he stroked his face, he couldn't feel his nose, then he tried to touch his lips, but he couldn't find his mouth. He looked around as if searching for an answer. The manager, from beneath the last table, takes out a pistol and fires four times into Rodolfo's body.

in time's cramped apartment

for Angel José Fernández

At this moment his wife is probably becoming anxious because it is already past eleven and he usually arrives home punctually at eight or at eight thirty. On those days he buys pistachios on Hidalgo Avenue; and even his wife knows that since it's now eight twenty Arturo will bring home some pistachios and with those pistachios he'll give her a sly and witty smile before settling down in front of the television. It has been two hours and fifty minutes since his wife thought Arturo would bring home pistachios and then we would sit down to watch *Rat Patrol* and *The Domecq Hour*; taking advantage of a commercial I'll put his slippers on my sweet Arturo and I'll serve him his reheated meal and maybe he'll caress my cheek and give me a kiss. But the truth is that several hours have passed and she repeats over and over I'll see him come in with his little white bag, we'll sit down to watch TV and, then, if he kisses my neck I'll invite him into the bedroom without watching *The Domecq Hour* and, as always, I'll remind him that the light will not be turned on and I'll not scream and no biting will bruise his back; in short, Arturo, I'll not see you naked nor will I let you look at my breasts which you have only seen by accident when I leave the bathroom or when I put on my nightgown to go to bed, the breasts that for thirty years you resisted stroking, but, with the passing years, it's no longer important to me or never was, sweet Arturo, provided I feel your spasmodic jerking and your semi-furious convulsions, despite the fact that your hands remain far away, buried in the sheets, trapped between your body and the mattress, repressing the caress that surely they wish to afford these lonely nipples, now flabby and wrinkled from disuse, tucked away, like the questionable jade earrings that I have never put on for that oft-mentioned party you promised me ever since we were first married. The party where we would be just as distinguished guests as any of those gringos who are stoned or high on marijuana and who come in and go out through those stately doors you open to them and who you continue to put up with despite the pestilential smell of digested partridge on their breath, but likely it has never bothered you considering their disgustingly abundant tips, their disparaging treatment of you, their contemptuous looks, and given the way you remain silent to the advances of some odious homosexual. So, sweet Arturo, that is why I have these nipples tucked away in the jewelry box of time; but it no longer matters, Arturo. Besides, now, at this moment, I cannot tell what I feel for you, if I feel sorry for you or if I loathe you. I cannot tell.

For a woman, being three or four hours late means burnt rice or soup that has boiled for hours and hours until all that remains are charred noodles stuck to the sides of the kettle. After the alarm goes off at six thirty, the warm soft-boiled eggs, herbal tea. Just right. In short, after your life is over in all its stupefying torpor, a dullness that is discussed for fifteen minutes over this or that, racing against the clock between the supermarket and an over-ripe tomato, yes. After being three hours late, you find a way, through that same numbness, a fissure that forms in the bosom of a woman's obsession. And it seems so great that in this house-bound monologue one would ask why this herbal tea with its few drops of lemon, why so many soft-boiled eggs and mended socks; her count was based on the multiplication of small acts: five years of one thousand five hundred to one thousand seven hundred soft-boiled eggs, in ten years at least four hundred pairs of patched undershorts, in fifteen years seven thousand comings and goings to and from the market; besides, those figures should be multiplied by six or three or two, depending on the situation. And now, now that she knew she was sitting on his couch, the one he gave her for composing his biography, an internal heat began to boil over in her and was escaping through that fissure, provoked by the inexplicable absence of Señor González.

She began by knotting and untying the dishcloth, then she chewed off the corners of her apron, she walked several times from the kitchen to the bathroom, and finally she flopped down on Señor González's couch. Time and again, she went over in her mind how he would arrive. Soon she couldn't resist spelling out a few dark passages that went far beyond the retelling of commonplace torpor. Her detachment gave her the strength to unloose her spiteful internal babbling, but the not-knowing-what-to-do with respect to that detachment also gave her the green light for what she would later call the dark passages of my life. Sooner or later it would have to happen. And probably it wouldn't have taken more than an hour and a half to give free expression to the trembling of her flesh and the obsessive gnawing of any rag or piece of cloth she might have at hand, but those were three strange hours, the three longest hours of her life and the three shortest and most painful hours because during those three hours she condensed, between memories and numbers, based on instantaneous mental pictures, the thirty years she had spent with Arturo González.

As for him, what Señor González never found out is that, after three hours of waiting, his wife had become quite relaxed, breathing quietly once the fissure in her bosom had been sutured, for the first time not turning on the television and seeming to watch some other invisible screen over the top of the sink. When Señor González went over and over that article from *Reader's Digest* he could only imagine that his wife would be chewing off her nails for a while, paralyzed, without being able to think about anything, until she fell asleep watching *The Domecq Hour*. It was for that reason that he told himself that Enriqueta couldn't help him in the least; besides, he knew for a fact that no one could give him a hand, not even he himself. He couldn't remember the moment when he raised his arms between the fourth and ninth floors, he felt responsible and satisfied, as if rested from a long walk through the center of the city. When he said satisfied he remembered again the precise passage from the *Reader's Digest* article, "among other potential murderers, should be included elevator operators, waiters, watchmen, bellboys, etc." And, perhaps, if the sentence had included him in the etcetera, perhaps the shudder of the first time might not have had such an impact on his forebodings, the obsession might not have grown or at least it might have been veiled within the infinite number of possibilities of homicides contained within that etcetera. But Dr. Scott had placed precisely one comma before the limiting etcetera, the word "bellboy." And there, in those seven letters, his name stood out, Arturo González, and those of all his companions. Then, in spite of the fact that he had always refused to apply what he called serious clinical irresponsibility to himself, he began to look into Felipe Caltenco, a young steward, sullen eyes, nervous hands and a dry mouth; he compared Roger Meléndez with Mr. Gray, an efficient hotel administrator for twenty years. He concluded that somewhere between the aroma of Mr. Gray's cologne and the smell of fried fish on Rogelio Meléndez could be found grounds for murder. Thus, with these meticulous observations, which in time would take on a certain mysterious sex appeal, Señor González discovered disastrous attributes in each minor hotel employee. Waiting, in any alley or dark corridor, was the razor that would slice open his abdomen because of some slight altercation a few days earlier. For that reason, besides the white gloves he ordinarily wore, he put on different ones—which he called security gloves—when he rubbed shoulders with his companions. That is how everyone realized, even though they didn't understand why, that he not only kept his distance from the guests and the administrator but also from the entire staff, including cooks and parking attendants.

His political discoveries were disturbing and hair raising, and so he'd say under his breath, as he returned to his apartment: that's right, it's disturbing and hair raising. In the last union meeting he attended, while bellboys, maids, waiters, stewards, and cooks discussed the need to go out on strike, Señor González thought: you're all a bunch of criminals waiting for just the right moment to gun down the guy next to you. And from the look on each of the faces, most of them dark, he found features similar to those of Goyo Cárdenas or Gonzalo Rojas, and even in the executive secretary general he found a hint of Margarito Zendejas. As a result, without realizing this growing cascade of premonitions, and unloading on his wife, his suspicions were confirmed by the slightest unusual action, the least ordinary or common nervous tic, the slightest wink of an eye. Seated on the little bench the sergeant had been so kind to offer him, the comings and goings of the photographers didn't matter to him or even what the reporters from all the papers congregated there might say tomorrow. The swarms of lawyers, personnel from the public prosecutor's office and their errand boys didn't matter either, in the isolation of interrogation by the district attorney's office. And he didn't know and would never know that at that very moment, more or less at eleven fifteen at night, a coincidence was developing between him and Enriqueta with regard to peacefulness, relaxation, and in the "it's all over for me."

Of course he didn't know and never found out that his wife was seated there with her legs impudently agape, letting the air that filtered through the little window of the dining room batter her flabby flesh, looking out, over the sink as if at a TV screen, due to a sudden break with reality. Someone approaching her at that moment would have discovered that the TV screen was inside her, under that place where her hair spilled over onto the back of the sofa. Señor González would never know, nor would it casually pass through his mind that at the same moment that Enriqueta was making her statement, the police recorder was taking down his (with a few spelling errors that no one would correct, writing down questions and answers, accusations and crimes, leaving out the invectives concerning parentage that Mr. Warners hurled at all Mexicans). No, he would never know about his wife's parallel version, her house-bound monologue that didn't stop until a hotel employee arrived to tell her about her husband's arrest, and told her to hurry. He never knew his wife went on watching the TV screen until the late night sign-off on the imaginary channel, where another Enriqueta jabbered on and told them that that was the way her nipples had become, tucked away in the jewelry box of time, like grapes left in the sun to shrivel up like raisins, lost, from being exposed to the elements, waiting for just a few fingers, no more than ten. But it wasn't always that way for me, that's why I have my little secret, a tiny one, but still a secret, Arturo, my Arturo, because you are not aware that once I pushed these same breasts into Mario's mouth, the eldest son of the doorman, yes, the son of the doorman. I plunged them into the mouth of one of the members of what you call the cult of murderers or taciturn, homicidal maniacs who lay in wait around the corners of any hallway. I poured out the pieces of my flesh that you had shunned, shunned as though they were one of your old issues of *Life* magazine, into the hands of a member of that very group, and if you want a real Enriqueta, here I am. It had to happen to me some day, because I could no longer continue fondling them in my own hands, waiting uselessly for a band of your murderers to ravish my body and, then, many thens later, resist the nonexistent attack of your rogues and satraps and then, then, enjoy melting beneath the odious hands of twenty vile types who never would have appeared. No, I couldn't wait any longer, my sweet Arturo. I provoked him myself, using my legs to my advantage, premeditating the use of my breasts, throwing my hot flesh onto him, so fast he couldn't even blink and then my breasts, my abundant hips, and if you want to know everything, I paid him, I gave him money to avoid ambiguity.

Mario stood in the doorway, so young, unable to understand that that morning there wouldn't be a garbage pail or old newspapers, not understanding that he wouldn't receive one peso but twenty or thirty or forty, Arturo, whatever I would like to pay him out of our savings. But don't think that it was all so easy, no, because at that moment when he knocked at the door with his timid hand, I was rolling around naked on the bed, like a bitch, shut in, fondling myself until I could have screamed out in pain, and if it hadn't been for that coincidence that I had hoped for so desperately there wouldn't have been anyone to blame. I said come on in, sweetie, come on, don't be afraid, and while I put the first twenty pesos in his pocket, my hand was already caressing his little thing. And later, for me, it was all so uncontrollable and hot, and right there, on the sofa where I'm sitting, I opened up my robe and my breasts fell out on his face and there was a little blood on the nipples and all manner of sexual misadventures—if you want to call it misadventures—then the little fellow turned into a wild beast. The youthful innocence of his face had disappeared, which meant that my Mario, Arturo, that my Mario had also gone crazy and docile and then his little appendage, without remorse, plunged into every corner of me and my mountains of skin and every inch of my body hair. That's the way it was, Arturo, we thrashed around on the floor, I screamed without a thought for our life-long neighbors or the fear that came over Mario. I gave him love bites on his legs, well that's what I had given him twenty more pesos for. That's how we spent the morning and later days passed and you never saw the hickeys and the bruises on my behind. My Mario never returned and the years passed and one day I saw him with his wife and children. I knew by the look on his face that our wild scene was going through his mind, while I remembered my thoughts from that time. I felt wet all over again to think that our experience together was just another adventure that he could brag about to his friends and I got even wetter thinking that Mario was probably exaggerating and saying that he had initiated everything, that he had forced me to yield and had almost forced me to stuff the mouth of this worldly man with my breasts and that his appendage and his body lorded over everything in apartment 18. From that morning on I felt like an accomplice to your murderers, from then on every time we went to bed I remembered every detail of that episode with Mario, his hands, his mouth, while you hid your hands, moving silently, with your face to the closet or to the window. Since then, I can assure you, I had sex with Mario and not with you, even though your hands would not caress as they wanted to, even though my nipples turning into raisins left out in the hot sun, even though you told me how much you loved me.

While Señor González was unaware of Enriqueta's situation and answered all their countless questions monotonously, he assured himself that he would never again poke around in the articles on the crime pages. It was no longer necessary. Not because a need for repentance gnawed at his soul, he wasn't at all repentant; moreover, he had no reason to be repentant of anything because he had confessed point by point that he couldn't remember at what moment he had raised his arms, at what moment he let go of the suitcase. He was convinced that he would never read the crime pages again. There was no need to corroborate the origin of thieves and criminals. He knew that all these articles would find Dr. Scott as their source: taxi drivers will continue to be both criminals and the objects of crime, accountants will murder their wives or will beat up their mothers, as is their custom; waiters will lock their daughters away for years in dark, rat-infested rooms; elevator operators, besides selling lottery tickets, some night will kill themselves with a bullet through the roof of the mouth in an evil smelling hotel room, after victimizing an unfaithful lover. Each one of those acts follows a preconceived command, they are motivated by a black hand that impels them to the obvious and commonplace result of murder and scandal. All you have to do is look them in the face, Señor González told himself, to realize that they aren't guilty, that there's no reason to get upset or feel repentant. On the contrary, after all those years of anguish and scrutiny comes peace, rest. Like now, with that contradictory tranquility that Señor González demonstrated while sitting on that bench, tired and sleepy and a little anxious for the secretary's typing and Mr. Warners' insults to end. Nothing made sense anymore.

Deep in thought there came to him, like a nostalgic anecdote, the image of the hidden corridors of the hotel. On the other side of these were the carpeted halls, the modest and recurrent wall coverings, the suites that, despite the clumsy aggressiveness of all hotels, reminded one of home. There was the bar and the restaurant, with furnishings and service that help guests forget, for a quiet moment, their urgency to visit the typical sites of the city; yes, there was the outside space, the visible face of good service. But Señor González was now immersed in thoughts of the mechanics of other hallways, the hidden face of the hotel, those service hallways where he and his companions walked, which were never seen by the clientele. While hidden they were necessarily naked, gray, starkly violent, but in the end, indispensable, just as almost all the employees were indispensable and efficient. And just like Señor González, they had understood that the hidden and visible faces, the truth and the hypocrisy of the hotel, were reproduced in their work and in their persons. Señor González was a prisoner of this reality for a long time after beginning work at the hotel: one night, after a day of convention activities of who-knows-what branch of private enterprise, Señor González began to walk through the adjacent corridors, beginning his trek home. He was tired, unwilling to open one more door. He went to the employees' locker room and didn't even want to wash up. He simply remained seated on the bench, next to the lockers, listening to the chattering voices of those who were finishing the first shift and the noise of money produced as the tips were counted. He fixed his gaze on Luis and began to observe the waiter's every movement: first he took off the waistcoat, next the thin black tie came off, then the shirt, and finally, surprisingly, Luis's jersey had a hole near his navel and another in the right strap, without counting four or five darns here and there. Next was Hernández with his socks all full of holes, the left one in the heel and the right one in the big toe. Ricardo showed up and, on checking his pants, he saw a matching pair of holes in the pockets. These images hit Señor González so hard he felt them take him back to the faces in the hotel, with its real and hypocritical halls, with rooms that conjured up warm feelings of home, and other rooms, like the one he was in at this moment, that reminded him of the city sewers. That's when he realized that they, Luis and Hernández and Ricardo and he himself, had their own hidden halls and sewers, their carpeted bodies and their gray and frankly violent naked bodies. While he leaned his head against one of the lockers, fear gripped him, an almost palpable fear because of its insistence, mixed with a growing smell of garbage coming up from the kitchen. None of the workers realized what González was going through, nor understood that González wanted to cry out in pity for himself and his companions and wanted to hug Ricardo's naked legs, wanted all of them to embrace each other in an orgy of solidarity, there, in the sewers, to share their different tears and pity, and be able to declare, shout out, what each one felt and thought of the others. Fear won out. González remained seated there for a long time, until the second shift began disappearing down the corridors. Later he became aware of his own nakedness. His movements were slow, lethargic, until he too disappeared down the hall that would lead him to Enriqueta.

Like the offices in any other police station, at table number four they were taking his statement. The typist produced a far different account from Enriqueta's. It was the account and reconstruction of the events that had jelled in ten minutes, in the five minutes before and five minutes after Señor González had lifted his arms. This had to do solely with reconstructing those ten minutes, which, because of Mr. Warners' shouting and swearing and Mr. Gray's constant interruptions, seemed like reconstructing a day of pillage and massacre. Even if, as Mr. Warners explained with great difficulty, the blonde woman wasn't really his lover, if in fact he had met her on Flight 203 and they had drunk a few gins together; if in fact he, Mr. Warners, wished he had not met her nor invited her to the same hotel, or at least hadn't wanted to accompany her to the hotel door; if in fact he, Mr. Warners, wanted and also didn't want a few of the so-called facts, he thought and shouted that New York was heaven in comparison to this underdeveloped capital, and besides that potbellied dwarf, that is Señor Arturo González, was a sonofabitch. As for the typist, in spite of being exhausted, she couldn't hold back a slight smile from time to time regarding the complications that no one could decipher. Because of the growing confusion, the statements were repeated for five hours—fluctuating between a calm version and one repeated ten times by Señor González, along with the "I never thought you would turn into's" of the administrator, and the announcement that Señora González had been notified. And for the ten life and death minutes the statement continued, not counting the months and years it would take to come to an end.

This time, perhaps the eleventh or twelfth, Señor González began again reciting with his tired and steady voice. As was his custom, he first opened the car door, he saw the blonde woman get out while he held the door. The woman stood up with difficulty, without noticing that she was showing off the entire length of her legs, including her black panties that the witnesses would later be able to observe. The accused continues: once the woman was shakily on her feet on the sidewalk, he thought she might be sick or drunk. The man he now knows by the name of Mr. Warners got out of the car and, as is typical with Americans, Mr. Warners told him to be careful, referring to the bags that the taxi driver had already placed in front of the hotel door. It is a fact: the blonde woman was drunk, so was Mr. Warners, and once Mr. Warners placed a tip in his hand, he blew a kiss to the blonde woman and then said a few words in English that the accused hardly understood. Then, after all that, she and he, Arturo González, went up the steps, the blonde in front and Señor González behind. They passed by the reception desk and Felipe told them blue section, room twenty-seven. As for the blonde, given her plunging neckline and the noticeably absent bra, who knows what things the accused said to her, because his sentences were a mixture of English and Spanish, because the words biutiful, jin, chingoan, beibi, aiam, cuidadou, etc., were heard. So they reached the elevator and no one else got on, for he remembers very well: once the elevator began its ascent the intensity of the light diminished, but after the light dimmed he just can't remember everything, because he only remembers that by the ninth floor he realized that the neck of the now deceased blonde was between his hands, and that one of her breasts, perhaps the right one, had fallen out of the front of her dress; that the body of the woman lay in a semicircle against the east corner of the elevator. He reaffirms it: he did not notice the neck of the blonde woman between his hands until the lady who lives in twenty-nine screamed out and he was startled by her, confesses Señor Arturo González. The lady in twenty-nine was waiting for the elevator with her husband. Finally, Señor Arturo González affirms that the husband of the lady in twenty-nine exclaimed, "Oh, my lord!" but that he didn't know whether that exclamation referred to the blonde's body or to what had happened. For some reason the accused cannot explain, the elevator went down by itself and the lady in twenty-nine screamed again at the moment the doors were closing. But once on the ground floor nothing was touched until the detectives and police arrived with their motley crew.

By that time the city streets were empty. A steady rain soaked the downtown streets. The few people who remained, pressed up against the building walls with hurried steps seeking the protection of the overhangs and entrances. From the doorway of one of these old buildings emerged a ruddy-faced woman about fifty years of age. A scarf covered her head, her lips were painted bright red; perhaps she wasn't aware of the rain or she didn't care if she got wet, because she was the only courageous person who didn't run or try to avoid the rain. She walked heavily, leaning a little to the right from the weight of a cardboard box she was carrying. After a few blocks the twine around the box would probably begin to hurt her hands. Perhaps not even that would bother her.

biological data

What is happening these days with heads of lettuce is a difficult thing to explain: quite suddenly they have taken on an unexpected and different form. It is so mysterious that it would be impossible for you to go to one of the many vegetable stands in the market and ask for a large, juicy-leafed head of lettuce . . . The produce lady would answer with an irrefutable air of confidence: Oh, don't you know what has happened to lettuce? Weren't you aware that they are in the process of complete change? Certainly, it would be the day's hardest blow. You should have noticed immediately that the biting laughter of the shopping ladies would be a marvelous introduction to any book by Kafka—to his discredit. But as you ripped up the first chapter, you wouldn't doubt for a minute that the frown on Don Pepe's brow formed part of a real plot, and that the introduction lay quietly waiting a few pages back. Immediately you would imagine that this embarrassing situation had been perfectly planned (a very bad trick); one in which children were small gears in that clock-like machine that carried the title: *The Little Boys Have Left Their Car and the Little Girls Their Jump Ropes, to Place in Doubt the Real Need for Lettuce*. You would also read on the following pages about strawberry and artichoke stands: *So without a doubt, Ramón Noyola Gómez, they were waiting for you to point out the grave inconsequence of your not being well informed about the constant, day-to-day changes*. For a minute you would be confused, but only for a minute, because by the third chapter you would think to yourself: This morning has fallen apart in my hands, and the breasts of the young lady in red have become eternally old.

The market spits you out as if manipulating the movements of your legs; you put up no resistance: you walk away. On Plan de San Luis Street, plowing through half the surface of the book, you will say to yourself angrily and yet nostalgically: I am a good-for-nothing imbecile. This part of the book will seem the thickest to you, then you'll realize that since you left the market the majority of the people who have crossed your depressed path looked insistently at you, as if yours was the only presence on that street. All of a sudden fatigue engulfs you. You sit down, without argument, on one of the benches in the garden you've come across; at that very moment the page turns, ending the sixth section. You will feel as though the agile footsteps of time are wringing you out, that in alliance with the heads of lettuce and the book they have made you age prematurely and that wrinkles, like a cracked windshield, have invaded you. You will not be able to explain what to do with your surroundings; you think about laying the text aside and just walking away, but the book that is on your knees captivates right up to the last word. You will immerse yourself in the seventh section, you will read that the old couple seated in front of you has been observing you since you plopped down on the bench. They continue to look at you tenaciously; you will have to get up because their gazes have penetrated to your lungs. Your breathing will become very rough; anguish, announcing with a shiver that you cannot stay there, will penetrate your backbone. The confused state that previously presented itself during brief moments now triumphantly enters into the expanse of your entire existence.

When that confusion crossed the border of your skin, you remembered the ringing of the phone in the night; the hollow voice of the apparatus could not awaken you completely to the cold dawn. That has gone on who knows how long; they said something to you about lettuce. You wish you hadn't gotten mad and hadn't thrown the phone down so hard: shit, you shouted.

In the last chapter, due to the finite nature of things, it was necessary to continue out onto the virgin pages of the text, the section entitled: *Without Him, She Stays at Home*. At this high point, you find yourself slightly out of sorts, as if a giant dipper of molten steel were poured upon your head. It appears to you that the letters have taken on life. Alive, they will throw themselves at your eyes like crabs, they will force you into thinking about the harmony of your home with the intent of grabbing onto any object, whatever it might be. But the whole thing is structured like a honeycomb and it is useless to hold out your arms to your beloved wife, followed by your children. Isolated thoughts rob you of your conscience. One follows the other quickly like the frames of an old silent movie: My wife is going to nag me about it the rest of my life: I don't know why I ever married you. She will buy separate beds, she won't pay any attention to me at all. I'll be worthless, she'll stop loving me forever. A substitute lover. My children will never forgive me for the lettuce. When they're grown up they'll make fun of me behind my back. I'll be the excuse for their nighttime escapades. Damned old man. They will be the butt of their friends' jokes. They will hate me forever. Even the people at the office will despise me. Poor Mr. Noyola, he's such an idiot. My boss will want to give me the elevator operator's job so that everyone who goes up or down can have fun at my expense. I'll retire without a single friend. Meanwhile, the heads of lettuce will have gradually become extinct. The last surveys done say you can only find their aroma. And even that, only occasionally.

the keeper of the keys

If it hasn't happened to you already, you can be sure that it will not be too long before you hear its infernal tinkling: All of us, at some moment in our lives, will inevitably run into the Keeper of the Keys. We don't want to imagine that this individual, as a child, felt a strong attraction, overwhelmed by uncontrollable forces, for the copper key in his grandmother's glass china closet; nor that the old keyhole in the front door of her house to him was a fierce and wondrous eye through which, more than merely looking, he spied on the neighborhood, nor that during long nights he suffered a lonely confinement, locked up by his absent mother or while in the adjoining room she gave herself over to the voluptuous pleasure to which every woman has a right. Neither do we wish to imagine that at fifteen years of age the Young Keeper of the Keys was already a full-grown man drawn toward arithmetic riddles and the indecipherable order of objects in a dark room, a circumspect young man, with a fierce gaze, not given to spontaneous smiles or to adolescent adventures; therefore, we shouldn't imagine that by then he had already accumulated an enviable and well-classified collection of the most extraordinary keys. It is likely that things didn't happen precisely that way and, perhaps, the key wasn't copper nor did it belong to his grandmother, nor did the keyhole belong to his mother's bedroom, and the collection was an ordinary bundle. Most of all, it would be unjust for us to approach such an intimate and secret biography as if it were the world's smallest keyhole.

But we certainly can suppose that key rings played a decisive role in this man's childhood.

In fact the only certainty that we can count on is his conduct, his current habits. The Keeper of the Keys has the avocation of a warehouseman, a cashier, an auditor, a doorman, a secretary, and of any office or profession related to an internal or external comptrollership. The position he occupies will depend not only on his preferences for control and optimum budgetary management, his social status and his vast knowledge of metallurgy. It will also depend on the "contacts" he was able to establish in diverse student clubs in which he was an outstanding participant, and also in the different organizations in which he has functioned and from which he has always emerged "smelling like a rose."

He makes his appearance at the office almost always at the workers' lunch hour. The conspicuous sound of his footsteps and the infernal clinking of the key ring that dangling from his belt, connected to the frayed, eternal leather strap announces that he will arrive within a few seconds. Before approaching his desk, he glances toward the timecard holders, the shelves, and the time clock, the cordex, with the gaze of a lynx, as well as at the employees who, with stuffed cheeks, would like to hide the bit of sandwich or cheese taco that someone has furnished today. He asks in a loud voice if there are any messages for him, and he always greets the crowd with the same loud voice.

The first thing he does is to take out a second set of keys, usually also attached to his belt by a small silver chain that he ceremoniously places in the left-hand pocket of his pants. He selects the smallest key with which he opens the two locks of his briefcase. He extracts a mountain of folders, receipts, accounts receivable, blank checks, and leave-of-absence slips, which he organizes methodically upon his desk. Later, from a small pocket sewed underneath the top flap of his briefcase, he pulls out another key ring and agilely inserts them into the various office locks.

Rapidly he sets out paper and carbon paper, pencils and felt-tip pens, erasers, correction paper, paper clips, and the latest memos and institutional newsletters.

He is obsessed by his control over the use of Scotch tape, a stapler, or a two-hole punch, highly prized objects for optimum departmental operation. He argues about the three cents that can throw the petty cash fund out of balance. His authorization for leaves is accompanied by the systematic investigation of the intimate life of the person who proposes to take care of a personal matter outside the confines of the office building. He loves to accumulate documents that carry the signature of all his superiors, with whom he is both condescending and accommodating, since he has the ability to anticipate the hidden meanings behind their apparently banal statements.

But he places his greatest effort in the area of his subordinates. If Martínez, let us say, does not address him using his academic title (even though at times he has not earned one), or does not address him in the formal manner, beginning with "Mr.," you can be sure that Martínez will have a tough go of it, because he will have to go around borrowing carbon paper, correction paper, and other useful items. The Keeper of the Keys will deny him the page sorter, accusing him, by saying, "You're behind in your work," or alleging that the sorter is out of order. But the most terrible thing is that Martínez will receive less and less work, they will freeze him out, the secretaries will give him the smallest piece of birthday cake, and in the end he will be totally ostracized. His tenure in that office will be brief and not even the union will be able to do anything for him. At that fateful year's end he will have to live through the most bitter of all Christmases, without a bonus from the Keeper, who will use complicated and deceitful bureaucratic red tape to snub him.

Like the inflexible caretakers of the eighteenth century, our man eventually surrounds himself with a halo of mystery, his skulduggery provides him with a coffer of savings that becomes a pretext for lending money at exorbitant rates. His conspiring ways, above all, permit him to presume that he manipulates valuable information. Even when he isn't the boss, he will be found "chatting" behind closed doors, being secretive in the corner office or in any hallway of the building, shifting his fierce gaze in all directions. His actions will even make the messenger boy tremble with fear.

The person who uses the first names of high officials and dares to answer the red, gray or black telephone is no other than the Keeper of the Keys. The loudest, most confident, and sonorous voice belongs to him. The person who stays after normal working hours doing "day-before-yesterday's" job, who can it be except he and a witness? This chosen one, just by luck, will get the most vacation time. He is the one for whom changes in administration mean nothing. The Keeper of the Keys is, in a word, the most solid pillar in our modern, simplified, and dynamic bureaucracy. Since childhood he has kept the magical key in a secret pocket of his pants.

the keeper of the shadows

It was nine o'clock at night and darkness was descending upon the buildings of the capital. A good share of the businesses had already turned out their lights and were now immersed in shadows, while others were beginning to close. The office buildings were also silent, without the shuffling of papers and notes, without the sound of typewriters or the ringing of telephones. Muted loneliness covered shabby desks and shelves; coffee cups scattered throughout the large work areas, as if their owners had suddenly abandoned them in an inexplicable emergency, as if life had refused to prolong itself in those places. But not all of them were empty, since there were some people, perhaps strange people, maybe a little crazy, perhaps very responsible—who knows?—who linger in the offices, without the courage to abandon them totally. Inevitably, they are in the habit of living many long hours behind their desks. And it would seem as though the world had assigned them to preventing a sense of melancholy in the file cabinets, drawers, swivel chairs and rugs.

Rows of office furniture extend into the distance, each holding up its own mountains of paper. In its nocturnal permanence, the office space opens up as if to infinity, where time stands still in the expanse of a timeless night. But in a certain corner of this labyrinth of partitions is found the Keeper of the Shadows, still fresh in appearance, wearing a diagonally striped tie with an impeccably white shirt, and a suit of requisite conservative tones. A man who commonly is of a darker complexion, thin, a little homely due to his offset nose or because of puckered lips that disfigure his face. He looks intensely at the expanse of his desk top, simulating one of those far-too-realistic modern sculptures.

At a certain moment that evening, while his employees and fellow workers were leaving, and the secretaries were giving the final touches to their cheeks before clicking shut their compacts, he, the Keeper Of the Shadows, picked up the telephone receiver, called home, and explained to his wife that he would be home later, not to hold dinner for him, to call him at the office if there was any emergency. But his wife, of course, would never call him; she was well aware that her husband was always there, on the other side of the capital city, in that immense office. During the first years of marriage she would call him, first because of inexplicable jealousy, then from the childless boredom that encompassed her and, finally, when the children were born, out of curiosity. Then one day she stopped calling at all. She would wait for his daily phone call so she could go on with her housework, putting the children to bed, rewarming the leftovers, removing the makeup that her husband never saw, waiting for the sound of the key in the door, watching television, and pleasantly greeting the Keeper of the Shadows. Of course, in the final analysis, he was a good man. On weekends they would go out to the country—they even had two cars—sometimes he'd take her to the movies, to the latest show. At office parties, he would proudly introduce her to his office mates. And on these occasions, she would admire him, since her husband always had a clever anecdote to tell or some expert comment on just about anything; he was knowledgeable due to his constant reading of the *Compendium of the Year's Important Happenings.*

Furthermore, he, The Keeper of the Shadows, has always prominently displayed photographs of his wife and three children on his desk. Which is to say, he accepts the idea of being a married man.

After that dusk-darkness phone call, The Keeper of the Shadows walked around saying good-bye to his employees, whom he calls "my people," and the other office mates, until finding himself alone amidst the deepening shadows, since the Janitors begin to slowly shut down the unoccupied and empty sections of the building until they finally reach our man's area, and he begins to occupy that infinite space of the immense, timeless night. As ten o'clock approaches, from outside the office, he studies a document that he almost knows by heart which he calls "my project." Then, on cards and little pieces of paper he sketches the outline of women like those found in women's magazines, outlines that he learned to draw from a manual that might be entitled *The Feminine Face in Ten Easy Lessons,* or else he recreates the characters from the comic strips of his youth to give them to his youngest child, or he practices his penmanship, or he writes interminable lines of numbers. But what pleases him most is to simply extend his arm, holding the yellow pencil, in a writing position, his eyes glued to the desk top, or looking at the large windows as if they held in their panes a grandiose, miniature world that can be understood only at night. And he doesn't get impatient: "stay calm" is another of his fundamental principles.

In his not too distant youth, he was already a refined and formal gentleman, distinguished, elegant, genteel. The bosses under whom he worked, on many occasions, suffered personal embarrassment when they were mistaken for his subordinates. That was when he acquired his nocturnal habits, since they represented "a point in his favor," as he would say in an attempt to convince "his people," in reference to the work systems espoused by his bosses. Of course, in time, this attitude served him very well. He came to be the Department Chief, then Vice Director, until, years later, he was promoted to Director upon the unexpected resignation of his predecessor. The Keeper of the Shadows lasted six months in the job—probably the most glorious period of his life—until, unfortunately, there was a change in administration. With a single blow he returned to his former position as Department Chief, the same hierarchical position that he now holds. Since that time, his wife admires him even more, although with a certain secret sadness, when she sees her man's efforts and patience.

In spite of that abrupt demotion, he continued dressing with the greatest degree of neatness, his manners were gentlemanly and he never complained about anything; his conversations continued along the lines of the wisdom of the compendium, with which he had become enamored because of some blabber-mouthed uncle or a decadent grandfather who had been a public or private administrator. The habit of "earning points in his favor" continued until ten o'clock at night every working day. He knows for certain that his bosses will return to the office after working hours to attend to any problem that their many responsibilities have not allowed them to resolve previously. Or that the sliver of light under the door of his immediate boss or his boss's boss suddenly becomes a large rectangle of light and smoke, while he hears voices that laugh and converse congenially and are transformed into three or four men carrying briefcases as they leave, while one of them breaks away from the group and approaches the partitions that surround the sculpture that represents our man, who hears his boss say:

"What are you doing here at this hour, Rodríguez?" while he pats the shoulder of the Keeper of the Shadows, saying good-bye so he can catch up with his colleagues.

"I was just leaving," he says to no one, since his boss or his boss's boss is no longer listening.

The Keeper of the Shadows turns his gaze back toward the windows, still thinking that the boss may return at any moment. His arm will remain extended as if he were writing. With the dark sky over the capital city the ten o'clock hour arrives; Rodríguez will get up from his swivel chair, he will button the second button of his grey coat and, with distinguished, secure footing, he will head toward the wife who awaits him.

lenin and soccer

You see, if you don't become a coach, you go into business or make commercials. Maybe you haven't seen Reynoso doing commercials for Bimbo bread, or the Bird Man advertising watches that are being knocked around by the ball during a phoney sandlot soccer game. I've stood right beside the Bird Man's goal and have never seen him wearing a watch—even knee pads bother him. Today only sissies like Calderón wear knee pads and watches. I came to the point of wearing them once, but I've grown up, and now just bare knees and nothing else, ol' buddy. But the thing that's really pissing me off and has me all screwed up didn't happen overnight. Besides, you know very well that soccer players past and present have always complained, and it's always the same old song: there's no security and it is all a question of luck and whether your legs hold up. Another thing that made me think about it was the SUTERM union movement. They've really pulled off a sweet little deal. Of course I'm not trying to squirm out of my responsibilities or discredit what the newspapers said about my anti-management campaign. And I'm not trying to get out of this because I believe that we were right, ya know what I mean? I thought about it for a long time and I even read a book by Lenin that talked about unions and what bastards all bosses are. Later on the idea began to mature in my mind like a good play on goal, and when I started my campaign, that lawyer, Iturralde, said that after the Tupamaros all we needed was a pinko, leftist soccer player, as if we players were nothing more than a bunch of kiss-ass conformists.

Benítez, who had sold out to management, argued that at least (just think, bud: *at least*) they were now paying better than before, better than when Dumbo Rodríguez and Fuentes the Pirate were playing. There was no reason to create such a scandal. But Benítez has already been brought up from the minors. He doesn't give a damn about what happens to the farm teams. Benítez never thinks about players on the second- or third-level teams. Benítez earns a good salary, has a sporting goods store, lives like a fat cat and acts just like the lawyer, like the asshole he is. Yeah, even though he has a Spanish last name he's Argentine, but the type that says that we have to finish off all Communists; yeah, he'd fit right in with the military, even if you don't believe it. Benítez, of course, can't really help it, and I'm sure he hates me because in all those meetings I used him as an example of what a soccer player shouldn't be. Elvira was afraid, too, but it was a different kind of fear—a woman's fear—although you might think that Benítez's fear was a woman's fear, that fits him even better. Elvira came right out with her don't get into trouble, just think about the children, they need a solid future, wait for a better time to bring this up and blah-blah-blah, and even in bed she kept on with her blah-blah-blah, hammering and hammering.

You know how sentimental women are, and Elvira turned out to be one of those radical ones, you know her. But I still appreciate how she comforted me at night when I was so desperate. Everything is going to be O.K., she'd say, in spite of the fits she'd throw in the morning, and her hands would rumple my hair and then smooth it back down. When she'd come at me with her tirades I wouldn't say anything, eating in silence, holding back the urge to blurt out my usual sons-o'-bitches. Elvira never took the time to think about things, the only things that existed for her were home, children, and her mother.

And my mother-in-law really did raise hell; my father-in-law, on the other hand, agreed that it was necessary to unionize the soccer players.

And I planned it all out, buddy, like I was selecting the very best national team. Just think, some of the players only wanted to ask for salary raises and extra bonuses. The ones I talked to were not only asking that all players be paid fairly, but insisted that it was important for us to create an organization that would protect us now and in the future. That would be the best way for us to gain respect, a soccer players' union. That was the only way that we'd have enough power to get them to stop screwing us over, all the way from level three up to level one. We formed commissions to go out to the provinces: we made a few converts in Toluca, and in Guadalajara they decided to go with the program all the way—that is, all the way to a strike if necessary. Even Gómez went so far as to commit himself to forming a good team that would go after management behind the scenes.

There was a reporter who promised me that if we put it all together he would publish some strong articles in our favor; that it was high time that sportsmen were treated fairly, that starting with us there was the possibility of creating a great confederation of sportsmen. And just remember that the articles were published but they went against us, screwing us over, calling us agitators and arguing that politics and sport were like water and oil. And that's when Elvira really went nuts, sending the kids off to her mother's place because, according to her, it wouldn't be long before they did something to us. Look buddy, I know that journalism works only by infusions of money and that the abuse of so-called honesty doesn't mean a damn thing to the Iturraldes of the world nor to the sports writers either; and yet, you become discouraged, not just because you don't have money to line the journalists' pockets, but also because the world starts coming in on you from all sides and no one will help you, and little by little even the people you trusted turn their backs on you. The reporter's very words were "some strong articles in our favor," which led me to believe that those articles would come out on the front page with photographs of the guys who were on the Committees, but no way, buddy. It was just a trap and it caught us all.

In the game against Pachuca, the center forward and Red Pérez were really pounding on me, as if they had been told to work me over, as a warning. I believe that they were told to do it because they would say, take that, you bastard, for being a rebel, under their breath.

They had to throw Red out during the second period. When I jumped to intercept a pass, he elbowed me in the ribs, right where everyone could see it. You know that there are always two factions that form, better yet, three. And the most dangerous players are thick as thieves with the boss, even though they're your own teammates. They can count on the power of money, in the form of bonuses, compensations, checks that seem to fall from the sky, and ignore the threats leveled against them. The same thing was happening to other members of the Committee; their own teammates would stab them in the back time and time again. In the beginning, no one backed down—they really had balls. In the end, only a few of us remained.

Why? Well, this is the way it all went down: three factions developed; management, who were the majority; those who were only asking for a salary raise, who were also a pretty large group; and us who, after all the hassles and name calling, were no more than twenty guys. At first it looked like we could count on more than a hundred players; everyone said, start the petition and we'll sign it. I agree, I agree. Everyone. But when the petition was circulated with all the economic and political demands, only twenty guys signed. Then at the Arbitration and Reconciliation Meeting they all went just to make fun of us. The petition failed and the chance to create the first national soccer players union went up in smoke. At any rate, we thought that we couldn't just leave things as they were. We had to exhaust any and all opportunities: continue with the campaign and begin to unionize at least one team. That way we could set the example and show that it wasn't a big deal, that nothing really big was happening, that no one would die in a battle like that.

You see, there were plenty of ideas to kick around. Right from the bottom of the league the guys need to have some money to take home; first, because they aren't students and they want to earn a living with their feet and, second, because they're confident that soccer is the ticket to fame. No one can make them believe that they won't be the Borjas of the future. They prove themselves on the farm teams' farm teams' farm teams, and if by chance they make the majors, they only get enough for travel expenses and a little pocket change. When they give you a contract, it's chicken feed, not even minimum wage, you just get taken. And then they want you to play for the love of the jersey—that's stupid. Soccer players are laborers just like anyone else, and that's that. Usually, you try out with the team that's been your life-long dream and that's when you get your first shot to the head: that's right, buddy, you're a long way from being a real soccer player (I've listened to those blood-sucking managers). They don't even tell you nicely that you have this or that problem, that you've got to kick with your legs straight and then arc them forward in order to fall right, or be more careful with your right-angle kicks, nothing. They tell you that you're no soccer player at all, that you're the shadow of the worst ball player that ever lived. I've seen lots of guys give their all and play their hearts out for Calderón. Then, after you've played for years in the minors, hoping that someone will get hurt and that they'll have to put a cast on someone, you have to play against your dream team and you'd like to let a few balls go by just to let your team win. But you can't because your salary and your job are on the line, besides the fact that there are always two goalies behind you waiting for you to miss or to get old, so they can take over. So you beat your team, what the hell, what can you do? After a while you don't have a favorite team, it's all the same to you if you're on the Necaxa team or the América team. The only ones who aren't soccer fanatics are the players themselves. That's what the fans don't understand.

One day, Zague told me the story about Amado Benigno, an extraordinary goalie. In 1926 he was the star of the Flamengo team. After a few years, he went over to the Botafogo team, and from there to poverty and, then, on to death. One morning he was found dead in the street. That guy was a world-famous goalie, Zague said. Zague also told me that in Brazil you had to be a Pelé for the government to support you when you got old. And as for me, meanwhile, I was thinking about the guys playing in the sandlots, and about the old guys who don't play anymore. Even though they aren't old, because you know that to management we players aren't worth shit. To keep playing when you're bald, you'd have to be an Escarone, or set up a little business on the side, or appear on TV advertising Bimbo bread, or get into any other kind of work that doesn't have anything to do with ball fields or stadiums.

Well anyway, once the petition failed, the idea of unionizing the team became an obsession with us. The idea was combined with other less important demands needed to convince a few more guys: paid vacations, full insurance coverage in case of serious accidents on the job, matching funds for retirement to be provided by each team you played for, etc. Some team had to go all out, and we were the first. Iturralde, the team lawyer, screamed his head off to management and came out with his unwavering demagoguery, saying to our Commission: you are not laborers, you're players, get this into your heads, play-ers. Not even his mother would have believed him. Our situation had become so desperate that no one could believe such foolishness, not Iturralde's ranting, not management's threats. If our political and economic demands were not met, we would go out on strike, no doubt about it. Leftist soccer players, that's all we needed. My mistake was to talk about the whole situation with Elvira, because her complaining and whining got worse and worse, and if we showered together she would keep on blubbering and bawling about her Home, her Kids, her Future. There was no way to answer her the way we answered Iturralde. I would lather up slowly, one body part at a time. I'd stick my head under the shower and leave it there for a long time. Elvira's words would mix with the sound of the water, and that way I'd get a little peace, ya know. Now Elvira is living with my in-laws. My mother-in-law has already hammered me about everything, the same lady who asked me so many times to dedicate a 'save' to her. My father-in-law comes and keeps pumping me up. Under his breath he tells me not to pay any attention to Doña Elvira, that sometimes she doesn't even know which end is up.

When management realized that things were getting serious, they started a smear campaign against us in the newspapers and on television. Threats and pressure tactics were the order of the day. Then came the real battle: some Mafia-types threw rocks at my house. Only one window pane was left intact, the rest were shattered to bits. We received anonymous cards and telephone threats. Elvira didn't wait a second longer; after the stone-throwing incident she left home. Then we decided to take the last step—go out on strike. Management left us no alternative. Even though they want us to come to the bargaining table now, management threw the first stone. The entire Committee couldn't sleep, but they never backed down. The strike became a reality. And right there, in the legal battle, now illegal, the whole thing began to fall apart. What happened then, ol' buddy, you already know by heart. The team changed its legal status, declared bankruptcy, and the Committee was left hanging. The suits against me came out on the front page, even though none of them had any basis. My lawyer turned out to be the slowest of all tortoises and I still can't see the end of the tunnel. I have a little money set aside: half of it goes towards the bond, and the other half for a taco stand or maybe a restaurant. And since I'm a real homely guy, they'll never give me a contract for TV commercials.

wind-up

As a rule, I like to live life's moments as if they were not occurring. That's what I do. Anyone can see that, when I don't think about the other side, when I walk around semi-pensive, half sleep-walking. The other side is this same side, the side of *logiké:* the inexorable side. Just to illustrate, let me cite the term *half-open*, which is not merely differentiated from the word *open*, but places us in a state of i-so-la-tion. There are innumerable people who leave *something* half-open. It doesn't necessarily have to be a door or a window; it can even be non-material objects. It's impressive being on the brink of what's half-open; the very act produces both participation and absence.

I'm walking down the same old street. Unexpectedly, it stops raining. The sun pulls its rays from its sleeve, as this heavenly body usually does, like the good celestial magician that it is. That's precisely its purpose: it sticks a hand into its top hat to pull out flowers before everyone's eyes. Not only do I discover this earthly magic show, but I also realize that there on the asphalt stands a parked milk truck, one of those painted with white bubbles. There in front of the mechanical cow is her dream, poised before a camera held by a human biped. I'm sure that it's an obstinate nephew who for months (due to his father's insistence) has been determined to drive one of his uncle's trucks. That commonplace description of the milk vender and his relatives is of no interest here. What catches our attention is the entire spectacle, all that is conjugated within that space street sky and within that time day afternoon, that infinite number of particles combined in a street's piece of afternoon. Above all, the prestidigitator and that gentleman with the thin mustache who was being photographed next to his property, one block before the path that has led me to the gateway to the road I am following right now. Yes, now I find myself annoyed on this side of the objects, anxious to imagine the other side of these people and these immutable buildings. Covetous of the young woman who just freshened her lipstick a few steps from me, that little woman who seems perfect for this story. I have only had this moment to penetrate her future imaginary body, her confident dance steps; one step forward, da-da-dum, a little jump backwards, da-da-dum. When she talks to her friends, even though she's a little reserved and not very out-go-ing. She must have a routine, of course, just as we have the subway each morning. In extreme circumstances—fatigue—if I didn't want to continue describing her, this would be a fruitless effort: she's about to begin walking away. She's an autonomous creature who has jumped out of my typewriter. She has escaped by some act of magic, untying the black and red ribbon from around her legs. In this case, I give in, I follow her inch by inch; I'll imagine her here wherever she may be. Of course I won't be there, but I'm sure that she'll be dragged behind me at a distance established by literary convention, which of course varies. I could be hidden in the bedroom with my portable typewriter and everything else, behind the wardrobe, so that—all upset—she'll think that the typing sound she heard out on the street continues even while she's in bed. Now, the lady has gotten ahead of me by a few pages. I'll watch her from outside the page.

I'll be able to see how she undresses with that freshness that sets her apart; the sound of the typewriter keys will bother her a little; it won't upset her as she takes off her skirt and her blouse. Everything proceeds without a hitch because I can see her even when I'm shut in among the clothes. If she should want to take out the clothes that she intends to put on after bathing, there wouldn't be any problem, because hurriedly I would write my own disappearance or, in case I didn't want to leave, who knows what would happen. The first possibility, upon her discovering yours truly, would be that she would scream like hell, that howl so common to women like her in a situation like this, if in fact it should happen this way. First her mother comes up, thinking that her daughter is having one of her usual dizzy spells. But with her mother's scream, her husband and her orangutan brothers would think something else; alert and on guard, they'd start coming up, one by one, according to their temperament, to attack me in a flurry of slobber and growls. If I still have a second wind, they'll turn me in to the proper authorities. The charges are: we have a warrant to search both house and home; damage to personal and common property; finally, reproaches from my own wife. Hospitalization—two months with a broken story.

She might see me out of the corner of her eye. She picks up her underwear, allowing me to see what color it is. She goes to the downstairs bathroom in search of a good shower; after getting ready, she'll eat her usual evening meal, her apparently unappetizing nightly meal. Her mother would notice something about her, since it's her obsession to *notice something* when it comes to her family. With a bean skin stuck to one of her teeth, she'd remark, I haven't seen those clothes on you since you went on vacation with your strange friends, do you remember? She would make one of her well-known gestures in answer to her mother's snide comments. Meanwhile, I rapidly write these things while asking myself what she'll do when she comes upstairs, fearful that she might instigate some sort of blackmail. I can't imagine any other alternative. Something like that seems imminent. If not, why has she acted in that fashion? Frankly, I don't know what could happen; she'll solve it all when she comes through the door. Only that creature, who has become totally independent, even from the writer himself, can resolve this quandary through her actions. I can't do anything until she finishes her meal. Maybe she'll be cynical enough to lose herself in one of the books that she's been reading for several days—Ginsberg or one of those—just to keep me suffocating in this closet along with my alphabet. That's what would happen from my vantage point, from her vantage point. Maybe she's just killing time until her parents jump into their newlyweds' bed of several years, and her astronaut brothers start masturbating while ogling *Playboy* pin-ups. But what we must agree on is that, at last she does come up the stairs; now you can very clearly hear the footsteps in the hallway coming from the upstairs bathroom. She has entered. Up to this point, nothing has happened. What's really extraordinary is what has happened since I've been in this bedroom. It's unusual that my presence should be sensed in this room of our "her!" The wardrobe doors, as can be plainly seen, are left ajar in such a manner that I'm able to see what's happening in here. I see that she's not at all surprised by a situation of this magnitude, by what the presence of my body represents. Perhaps she has come to realize what I represent to her rebellious monotony; then, I should get out the same way I came in. My very presence is enough to let her know that not everything can be reduced to an alarm at 6:45 and soft-boiled eggs on the run. At this point, as night falls, with everyone secure in his own little piece of darkness, *boom*, we get right into bed, all hands. All bodies. But no such luck; we've been talking about tons of problems that she's wanted to air out on anyone she could. She's no "special," I mean "exceptional," woman. She has certain philosophical blind spots, doesn't understand the significance of the all-too-often-mentioned "generic man of Feuerbach." I, on the other hand, have not been able to tell her much about that man; I've told her that he's a man of imprecise characteristics, more or less like someone without a surname and, even worse, without a first name. She tells me that in her youth she was involved in some communist party activities, but that now, after having read about a few epigones, is concentrating on an in-depth study of philosophical fundamentals which, she says, were the *quid* of the entire problematic. We discussed it until morning. She said she wanted to sleep for at least an hour. I went down the stairs cautiously. My face collided with the morning in route to the other side, carrying my typewriter.

She notices that I'm in her wardrobe, and is a little startled. She gives me a disgusted look, as if upset by my ridiculous position, squatting and with my typewriter on my thighs. We're accompanied by the music of Jethro Tull: *Wind-up* and *Aqualung*. Her first impulse is to take off running toward the toilet with an overwhelming desire to throw up; this comes upon her whenever someone appears. As a rule, it is writers who overwhelm her. This time she resisted it, she recovered from her dizziness and nausea by applying a violet-colored cream to her face. She opened the wardrobe doors. I felt naked: to tell you the truth, I felt ridiculous. But she gave me encouragement, wings to fly, by telling me to get out and sit down on that chair.

She tells me that whenever she's busy they appear. We discussed a few writers (she knows quite a few); she brought out something to eat; in the kitchen, the lady of the house told her that for days she hadn't had an appetite, and that it pleased her that she'd taken almost two helpings of leftovers. She congratulated her, finally, for she was no longer imitating men's voices like a ventriloquist. Martha laughs a little, thinking that the lady is really a nice person, and it couldn't be any other way. I ask her why she lives in a boarding house. She answers that people have asked her that millions of times, but that she has nothing against answering me; she knows her own history down to the last detail. She even tells me that perhaps no other girl knows herself like she does. Of course, her history is fairly commonplace. Not only because of the ghosts; but now that she has met me, that she has begun to condense me into one of the periods of her young life, everything was swirling about her in a great circle. I was spinning, my life was entering an extraordinary state; Martha is attacked by zigzagging guerrillas. She has told me that her surname is Covarrubias and that her father is none other than my very own. Fossilized memories come back to me: the Stegosaurus, Plesiosaurus and Iguanodon. A trilobite is crawling along with difficulty. It tries to catch up with its companions, pulling itself along with its crustaceous feet. At first we thought it was some coincidence, but when its voice fractured the sentences I, ta-da, understood: we were creating a biography in which both of us were immersed. I squashed the crusty beast with a rock; his animal friends have returned to the Devonian age. After realizing that we were united by a single penis, we said to each other, somewhat stunned, that when all is said and done it doesn't really matter: both of us have taken parallel paths. But on this night, we have found ourselves in infinity since that's where these parallel lines meet.

Our world is transformed into something bristly, the peacocks of our own lives, we see beyond the other's face. The rainbow feathers at our backs fan out into rock music. We have agreed to obscure what has been revealed, to outline our surroundings with thorns so as not to overstate the situation. For me, she was Martha, and nothing else, even if the disparity between us would shout out its here I am. I also said to her big deal, that having a half-sister who knows me doesn't mean a damn thing to me. The distance separating us has been covered rugs of variegated words, a winding road of letters. Then we created a bed out of words with double meanings; she expounded twisted ideas to me. I inundate her with ambiguities. In order to confound each other we install an illegible wall in this room. We knew that lovemaking was validated by irrefutable sophisms, thinking that morality is outmoded junk used by old aunts to disguise menopause. We accept barbed wire as the guardian of morality. But what does it matter, we're already on the other side, bleeding. We have built a different eroticism that attracted us like a lie attracts a cynic. We suspected that while doing it we were enjoying it in a peculiar manner; coitus, under these conditions, was like finding a winning lottery ticket on the street, but the police are there ready to throw you in jail for kidnapping a little orphan—we were content to look upon it as if it were fool's gold. Just as we tore up that ticket, Martha and I squeezed each other between the sheets, excited, fearful, with controlled arousal, biting each other until we bled. *Wind-up.*

the shadows

for Esperanza and Carlos

The quiet tree where the limpid autumn is enclosed within the depths of the patio

Li Yü (from trans. by Luis Roberto Vera)

The man is seated in his rocking chair at the door of his house. An oblique light strikes the houses across from his. On an afternoon like this, exactly three years ago, a woman died, the wife of the man in the rocking chair who, surprised at his own peacefulness, slowly rocks and remembers, amid frayed images, the avatars of his wife's funeral. He observes the branches of the lemon trees that emerge above one of the houses, the sepia-colored house. There, in the foliage, the autumn light produces a scintillating dance of tiny shadows and light. The leaves appear and disappear, combed by the calm autumn wind. Even though the man does not perceive it, or believes he only slightly perceives it, a leaf descends to join the other fallen leaves in the garden hidden by the house, there, behind the sepia color, the garden encircled the passageways that form a quadrangle of large flower pots and cans with tufts of juliets, azaleas, geraniums, spikenard, parsley, camomile, or peppermint. The man continues to rock, peacefully. His shadow assumes the mobility of the curved lines of his chair. He smokes, and the smoke from his cigarette outlines a new language in the air of the quiet and solitary street. Perhaps the ribbons of smoke have written the ideas the man begins to formulate. He watches the playfulness of the smoke and imagines a type of Chinese calligraphy that speaks with the wind and dissipates, leaving a message where the perishable predominates. And it all takes place as if a feminine finger were writing in gray letters: this afternoon will not be repeated because the next time the lemon trees will have grown a millimeter higher and the lady in the sepia-colored house will have cut the camomile, or the juliets, or perhaps the clouds that the man does not see will never return to create that oblique light that prints a subtle happiness on the leaves swaying in the sky. Besides, the feminine finger perceives that all those elements that have come together three years after her death will be like messages left upon the table that say that we will soon return, provided the man who reads the smoke of his cigarette does not decipher what happens in that slice of an afternoon. But there's no need to worry, because the man in the rocking chair already knows that he is at the center of the unrepeatable. And despite the fact that his meditation begins to stray from his shadow, the meaning will point toward the idea that the feminine finger draws and erases. The man perceives the mixture of scents coming from the garden of the sepia-colored house, which causes him to imagine the sprouting of the lemon trees. Then, it rises through the foliage until it blends with the swaying branches observed by the minute fauna that inhabit the tree. He feels the brush of the autumn wind and becomes inebriated by it. With something akin to vertigo welling up in his breast, the man observes the different forms his shadow casts on the floor, as if he were watching the landscape of his small-town street through his window, of which he also is a part.

"Our shadow reproduces our body," he thinks, without knowing what the next sentence will be, "but it upsets our body, makes it tentative, hides it, denies it in its darkness . . . "

Before going on, because he is suffocating, he inhales the aromas coming from the hidden flower pots and the tufts growing out of the cans.

"A shadow speaks through our body—we know of the latter through the former. It is the black messenger lark of our existence." The man is overcome by emotion, perceiving that a former time and space have entered into his being. "The shadow, as such, suggests, alludes, converses in the semi-darkness: it is the hypothesis of our life; no, it is not reality, although it assumes the same movements and curvatures of the rocking chair, or crumbles on the steps that we ascend, or accompanies us, dissolving and reconstituting itself against the windows, all up and down the street . . . "

Now, the man in the chair no longer feels stifled. His emotions have turned toward his thoughts; he is at peace again. He rocks as if he were traveling in a boat, floating, with no concern at all, upon the pale yellow waters.

"A true shadow never existed," he continues, "since it could never be identical to the man of whom it is but a cloudy message; it achieves an independent life, subject to laws that are not attributable to the body from which it originates, even though it travels with us as a mysterious friend who has lost the ability to speak. Consequently, my love, I know very well that the shadow devoid of woman that imprints itself upon the sepia-colored house was never your shadow. Yes, I understand that it accompanied you for fifty years, but it was only that, your tenuous companion. It had no reason to die when you left. You know that shadows do not perish because they never existed like a live body; nevertheless, they are full of the life of those for whom they were black messenger larks . . . "

The man continued thinking about other matters regarding shadows, as his cigarette went out. Little by little, the oblique autumn light began to lose its strength. The aromas disappeared in a vigorous autumn wind. The head of the man in the rocking chair fell to one side, as if he had suddenly sunk into a peaceful sleep.

Some of the neighboring people agree, others disagree, that it was pure invention, but they say that when the rocking chair stopped rocking, a shadow devoid of man crossed the street, scaled the sepia-colored wall and disappeared among the leaves of the lemon trees as night began to fall.

georgina, here and now

A horizon of shipwrecks
hope everywhere

Oscar Collazos

The house, just like that, quiet and cluttered, Catsup, the Nescao Carla's panties the cocoa cup with the strainer on top, spoons on the table, besides folders bibs a half-eaten apple, like that, with all things out of place and occupying forbidden spaces, with no music and no TV, only insignificant sounds coming up from the street; the house, just like that, seemed to Georgina to be an empty house, worthless, ready to fall down, dragging the rest of the building toward that uselessness. Despite that impression, Georgina's intuition told her that it wasn't right that the house should cause her such absurd feelings, she all but considered it contradictory, especially since she knew that the scattered objects represented life, even though they represented a past life and motion, and that they were only waiting for a hand, the dishcloth, the water from a tap and the tips of the washboard. Georgina had just come in from the street, from a diversity much more cluttered and incomprehensible, she had been thinking about the time when Bernardo put some Cuban cigars in the refrigerator, and he never smoked them because the fridge wasn't working properly and it froze too much and, then, after about a week, the cigars looked like sausages stuck in a tight plastic casing. They weren't bothered so much by the frozen fate of the cigars as they were by the fact that a friend had sent them from that island that sails, free, upon the waters of the Caribbean, and because it meant that the smoke that would have perfumed their apartment was also frozen. Then she thought that things like that were always happening to them: red wine with a pickled spider, the Saúl Karsz book with half its pages blank; and she could go on remembering those strange happenings that at first they enjoyed and celebrated and that later made them think of dirty tricks and jokes in bad taste. By way of some type of good-bad luck, society's bad jokes, the small ones and the large ones, like a laborer vomiting blood at daybreak, they were the sign of violence and bitterness, a sign that could very easily find its way into the tobacco of some frozen cigars, in a spider swimming in a bottle of wine, in a pitcher that broke when they put it on a shelf of the bookcase. Or the suitcase that was stolen in Córdoba, the one that was full of typical blouses and drawings of Guatemalan Indians.

Besides bringing together the rosary of their good-bad luck, Georgina remembered that Bernardo and little Carla would not be home when she arrived; they had gone to the circus so that she, Georgina, could do her things in peace. Alone and concentrating on finishing her review of *The State and Revolution,* she knew that upon arriving she would have to deal with their absence. But what she had least anticipated was that upon entering the apartment she would feel like it was on the verge of caving in, that it displayed a certain contradictory uselessness in the scattered objects. With a feeling of emptiness she began to pick things up; it would take only an hour to leave things in pretty good shape; at any rate, that was her designated allotment of time for manual labor; afterwards, Bernardo would add his hour once Carla's diapers were changed for the night and was taking her bottle. Furthermore, and she had experienced this on previous occasions, if she began working with the house in a mess she would not be able to concentrate, she would squirm around, uncomfortable at seeing things in forbidden places. So, she preferred tidying up, at least cleaning up the area where she would be working. Yet she always liked going a little overboard, not so much because she was a woman and because of the domestic traditions she had inherited from her mother—which were now falling apart dish by dish, garment by garment—but rather because she loved Carla and the new Bernardo. To her, going a little overboard meant returning love, a touch of affection, it was like giving a little kiss to the things that they all used, because love and affection didn't go away with the changes that had taken place between them, between her and Bernardo; she had to give them another meaning, a new impulse, freer, sincere, even though other eyes did not understand, even though to those supposed other eyes everything seemed formally the same, the same affection, the same kiss, the same bodies making love, because, after all, those supposed eyes would probably believe that if she were to show some affection toward another "man" it would be a cunning type of deceit, when all is said and done it would be a repudiation of that domestic tradition, maternal endurance in her eternal kitchen, with her eternal mop, her eternal bed, while the man of the house, always loved and forgiven by this patriarchal society, would while away his life in that eternal cantina, with his eternal morbid jokes, in his eternal other bed.

That's why Georgina, now, after cleaning the table where she would write her review, was hanging a white curtain over the hallway window, knowing that her extended legs, with her skirt reaching the edge of her panties, were well shaped, pleasing and caressable, according to references by Bernardo and a cat call or two from the streets; she felt as though Bernardo's eyes were resting on her calves and then she felt them run up toward her thighs and slip under her skirt all the way to her behind. She let her arms fall and with that movement her body relaxed after having been taut, Bernardo's eyes fell from her hips, disappeared from her imagination, and that was enough for Georgina to overcome that sense of a useless house, which had held her hostage until she hung the curtain. She told herself that it would be good to turn on the radio, listen to the news, a little music; she even gave the curtain a little tug, a final adjustment. She looked out the window, her eyes reaching out as far as they could see, taking in the naked rooftops of the houses in the area where a gang known as *Los Nazis* were the scourge of the neighborhood. She had heard in the butcher shop around the corner that many of its members had joined the ranks of the Judicial or Secret Police—actually, she never could distinguish between the Judicial and the Secret Police, but she knew that the Federal Police were more effective than the others. She remained there for a long while looking at the rooftops; because of the poorer houses in the distance, she remembered *Los Nazis,* with their frightening motorcycles and black leather jackets with the customary skull on the back, and daggers hanging from their belts and a phoney revolver and holster in the frightening Nazi leader's jacket pocket. However, regardless of the fact that she understood that poverty and exploitation were the terrible lifeline of these gangs—because one must remember that each poor neighborhood has its gang: The Bad Boys, The Crocodiles, The Big Daddies, etc.—she had proven that the newspapers and the television news programs avoided the mention of these gaudy gangsters in their antelope-skin jackets, rich brats converted into dangerous murderers and big-time traffickers: cocaine and morphine, arms and white slavery—"the houses in the affluent neighborhoods with gratings and flower gardens . . . there are pink ones, little green ones, little white and blue ones," she thought Víctor Jara would sing. That's right, the media disregarded the atrocities of the "little daddy's boys," of "the—real—seditious gangsters," just like they overlook many other atrocities, like a laborer vomiting blood after a beating. "There are pink ones, little green ones."

As she moved away from the window, Víctor Jara's song kept going round and round in her head, and she got that same sad feeling as always when she listened to his music: How many times had she cried over his songs, feeling that his voice, a little off key, showed more the need for revolution than the fact that they were out of tune. And what about the female laborer who is waiting for her man to return—"stand up and look up at the mountain"—hadn't it led her to who-knows-what bitter choices and sentimental mechanisms?—"stand up and look at your hands"—and to think, as if in a drawn-out nightmare, that the crushing of the Chilean people had been a gangrene that spread little by little from rumor to reality, difficult to stop with words and ideas, and that she understood it better when she listened to Víctor Jara's songs or read a story by Skármeta or Délano; and furthermore, feeling an immense anger accompanied by bitter tears, reading some damn poem by Nicanor Parra, thinking, even though bourgeois morality did not allow that in a woman, that all of the Nicanors were just a bunch of sons-o'-bitches, without any balls, well before the gangrene, well before the hooded and unhooded murderers, to always end up sad and crying softly, while Víctor Jara's song turned and turned, until all of this is resolved?

By then she had already turned on the radio, a waltz was coming out of the speakers. She wondered if the composer was an intrepid and always-loved-by-the-ladies younger Strauss or the authoritarian and jealous elder Strauss. Just think how many things happen to a person, she said to herself. We experience a varied table of life that tries to destroy us in its silence; we experience a curtain hanging in a window through which we are transported to rooftop cisterns and clothes on a line and the gangs and the little houses in the rich neighborhoods; we experience Víctor Jara and gangrene and then we experience the mysteries of the Strausses. And now Georgina, with ink all over her, checks off the contradictions of her life; finally resting from the tensions of the street and her home, she recovers the presence of Bernardo and little Carla; the clean table, all cleared now; behind her she hears the strains of one of the Strausses, she walks down the hall to *Revolution and the State,* to her green notebook. She sits at the table, picks up her pen, takes out her first reference card, and smiles.

"The Capitalist State is capable of assuming the most diverse forms, always preserving its essence, unerringly maintaining the social base of exploiting capital at the expense of labor. For that reason Lenin tells us: 'Democracy is a form of State, one of the variations of the State. And, therefore, it represents, as in every State, systematic and organized violence against the people.'" These sentences began the first draft of the review Georgina was preparing. She was responsible for the introduction to a longer study about the State that had to be turned in by the commission no later than a week from today; even though they had to decide on the structure of the document, Georgina was not at all happy that her section was to be called *Prolegomena,* neither did she like the word *Proem* that one of her comrades had proposed. She thought those words were somewhat overblown, prideful words that strolled comfortably along a boulevard lined with bush-words that, on the contrary, stir up controversy, rebellion, structural change; she couldn't understand how pride-words and revolution-words could ever coexist peacefully. She preferred, for example, that her section should simply be called Introductory Notes; the word *notes* eliminated all possibility of allowing *introductory* to be considered pedantic, as if a proletarian word should be able to exercise rigorous control over the word bourgeois; besides the fact that *introductory* was a more common word, even used by the classics, that is to say, it was more of a working-class word, one that had worked harder in the history of rebellious texts. When Georgina became aware of the digressions set off by her feelings toward different words, she felt a little embarrassed at what her comrades would think about the coexistence—or lack thereof—of words. Perhaps because of that same embarrassment, that comes over her from time to time, she had not wanted to get into a big discussion about the title of her section, and perhaps for that same reason she felt obligated, at least for now, to use the word *Prolegomena.* Besides feeling embarrassed, she became angry, because no one questioned or made fun of something she had not dared to bring up; she believed that this represented an example of self-repression: if they were accustomed to discussing so many unimportant things, why not discuss fully the title of her section? Then she asked herself if the term *profit motive* wasn't a ticking time bomb that had blown to bits all classical economic theory, and that functions today like a veritable stick of dynamite not only in the criticism directed toward bourgeois ideology, but as the supreme instrument for politicization and propaganda, somewhat like the idea that would end up one day as the trigger of a machine gun fired in anger and responsibility. Between the terms *profit motive* and *prolegomena* there could be no such thing as equality, because there was a huge disparity; therefore, Georgina concluded that the term *profit motive* should be accompanied by similar dynamite-words, words willing to offer the syllables of their lives. She picked up her pen, scratched out the word *Prolegomena* and wrote: *Introductory Notes*.

She reviewed the first paragraph and said to herself that that afternoon she had been inspired, that in her paragraph there was nothing extra or lacking, that the quote by Lenin fit perfectly, the way a person would speak of every day economic operations in his society. Why didn't people understand the ability of the Capitalist State to wear such an effective mask: the Milk Maid State, the Philanthropic State, the Clear Conscience State, the Spinster Church Mouse State. Georgina was swooning a little as she masked and unmasked the great buffoon, a dizziness caused by thinking about all the fools who were entertained by watching the great buffoon's mime show, sometimes ridiculous and other times frightening. He was equally expert under a broken-down tent as in the Palace of Fine Arts. Georgina was certain that at any moment the charlatan would jump down from the stage, take off his striped hat to put on a helmet, lay down his cane and replace it with a bazooka, show his true face, uncover the monster, and fall upon the unarmed spectators. Georgina believed that, due to the changeability of the great buffoon, it was vitally important to begin demonstrating that "The Capitalist State is capable of assuming the most diverse forms." In spite of the fact that at any given moment he might not attack the spectators, the mimicry, the modest staging, the striped hat, the old cane, all of these were elements that entertained the fools so that they would not become aware that on the other side of the canvas and outside the Palace of Fine Arts "the exploitation of capital over labor" continued unabated. Furthermore, the charlatan, shielding himself in his old-democracy cane, while the spectators heard last call and they supposed he was still in his dressing room putting on his makeup, was applying "systematic and organized violence against the people." Georgina's dizziness continued, due to a feeling of impotence and because she had discovered the identity of the person who played those dirty tricks on her and Bernardo; she knew that the tricks came from the great buffoon, and there really were no such things as coincidences or sudden occurrences; that all corresponded step by step to the somersaults, the guffaws, and the mimicry that came from a circus tent or the palace, circulated calmly throughout the city and settled in a bottle of wine, in a refrigerator, in a garden, in a factory, in a book, in the feeling that a certain house is empty, useless, in the word *prolegomena,* leading all the gangs in town—in the algae of a cistern.

She was so distracted, so intent on her work and thinking about the somersaults of the great buffoon, that night had sauntered into her apartment like Old Fido into his dog house, like a silent spy, without

Georgina even realizing. When she saw that the night encompassed everything, she remembered getting up to turn on the light in the dining room, but the absence of light had not warned her that night had surrounded the house—only that momentarily she had needed the light to continue working, that something strange was happening because the light was fading, as if by an oversight on her part the day should stay bright until the next morning. Because of that oversight, when she got up from her chair, stretched and yawned and went to close the hall window she had left open a few hours before, she was surprised that night had already fallen, peacefully, over the city and had entered into the apartment the way Old Fido enters his dog house, or like the silent spy who had been watching her while she composed her *Introductory Notes* and thought about the consequences implicit in the diversity of forms the Capitalist State might adopt. It occurred to her that Bernardo and Carla would arrive soon. She went to the kitchen, to the fridge, she took out a carton of milk, served herself a glass and drank it down promptly; out of the dish drainer she took a little pan, put it on the burner, this time pouring a double serving, thinking that Bernardo would also like some warm milk and that it would really be cool to greet him with some hot coffee and diet cookies arranged on a tray. She told herself that it was time to talk a little, because this business of not talking for so long would gum up your tongue, especially since she was known for being sociable and talkative. While the milk was heating, she leaned against the fridge, decided to talk out loud, and sang something that Carla liked: Baby, Baby, Baby mine, a little piece of Heaven oh so fine.

She was listening to a Bob Dylan album and drinking her coffee when Bernardo and Carla arrived. Among the blankets that covered her, Georgina could see Carla's little face, covered with chocolate or some other type of sweets that Bernardo customarily stuffed her with, even though he knew that the pediatrician had recommended giving her as few sweets as possible; premature cavities, digestive difficulties, concern about obesity were a few of the reasons. As soon as she saw them come in, Georgina smiled and ran to Carla's room to prepare the crib and to turn on the vaporizer—Carla had bronchitis. Bernardo carefully laid Carla on the mattress, untied her shoelaces, took off her shoes, and removed her socks for better circulation. Georgina turned off the light, and they silently left the room. In an exaggerated fashion

Bernardo exhaled as if he had been holding his breath for half an hour. They kissed.

"She's really getting big, isn't she?" Georgina said.

"Yes, she already weighs a ton," Bernardo answered.

"How did it go?"

"Fine. She was crazy about the elephants and hippos. Then she got kind of fussy, but it was still worth it to take her along."

"Did she take a nap?"

"No. I don't think she'll wake up now. As soon as she's fast asleep I'll change her."

They headed for the dining room. Georgina poked Bernardo in the ribs; Bernardo ran ahead a little to get out of her reach, then they came back together and kissed again.

"Do you want some coffee, with milk?" Georgina said.

"That would be nice."

"Sit down and I'll bring it to you."

Georgina went to the kitchen and brought the coffee pot; Bernardo already had the cup ready. They looked into each other's eyes and smiled. Bernardo took a cookie and bit into it, while Georgina poured a little milk in the coffee. And while Bernardo stirred his coffee, Georgina went on:

"I've been thinking about a whole lot of dumb things. Like being alone really makes me nervous. I miss you two."

"What were you thinking about?"

"What do you want me to tell you for, just dumb things."

"Were you able to work?"

"Yes. Maybe later I'll read you what I wrote. I called it *Introductory Notes;* I don't like that word *Prolegomena* very much. Don't you think it's a little outlandish?"

"I hadn't even thought about it."

"I had. I think that that's the way one of Father Berkeley's titles begins, right?"

"If you want to, just leave it like that. I don't think that's a problem."

"I also thought about the cigars and the spider in the red wine, as if they were dirty tricks that some idiot was playing on us. I don't suppose you've thought about that either?"

"Well, I haven't; but the fact that they're dirty tricks, well, they are. They didn't want to exchange the Saúl Karsz book—another dirty trick."

"And what about the wine bottle, ol' buddy?"

"And those were the dumb things you were thinking about?"

"Yes, among others. It's really funny how a person can think about so many things in just a few minutes, isn't it? Sometimes I think you live faster in your mind than in life. Or maybe it's insanity, who knows?"

"It could be both. And besides, you're half-crazy."

"Don't be a dope. What really bothered me was to find the house all torn up."

"We have to be more organized."

"Well, yeah, but sometimes you just can't do it."

Slowly, as they finished their snack, Georgina began explaining each of the ideas that had come to her while she was alone, ideas she had called dumb; though after discussing them so many times, they came to the conclusion that in fact they were far from being dumb. Bernardo congratulated her on her play on the presumptuous word and the revolution-words; he suggested that with that word play and the idea of the State as an underdeveloped Fred Astaire she could write a good story, that she should write it, that the worst thing that could happen would be that she would fail. Then Bernardo, a little tired and worn out from having dragged Carla all over, began to fold her diapers. Neither one of them noticed that the table and its surroundings had been invaded by all sorts of objects—Bernardo's jacket hanging over a chair, the diaper bag, the baby's cap, a couple of bibs, and some more of Carla's things in the easy chair, so that one could make an inventory filling pages and pages, including cigarette butts, barrettes, books, dolls, and bits of bread.

Georgina saw Bernardo disappearing into Carla's bedroom. It wouldn't take him long to change her, Bernardo was now as skilled at taking care of Carla as was Georgina, who was lighting a cigarette, the first one of the afternoon-night, and while she took her first drag, she flopped down on the sofa. Her eyes wandered over the living room/dining room, and didn't care about the clutter—she felt tired and happy. There, on the sofa, where she could look out the picture window to the street, she would wait for Bernardo: she'd invite him to make love, then they'd stay in each other's arms for a good while, maybe they'd sleep until daybreak, and then bleary-eyed from sleep, they would go to bed, since they always made love in the big chairs, without their underpants. Georgina smiled and continued smoking, letting the smoke escape from her mouth as if the cigarette were burning all by itself in the ashtray, circling around her face, rising from her large, fleshy mouth, curling around that straight, sharp nose, filtering through her eyelashes, her white skin disappearing and reappearing among the hollows left by the tiny smoke rings that danced upon her face. She sat up, stretched out her arm to the ashtray, and flicked off the ash. When she lay down again, another smile formed on the face where the smoke had been playing: sometimes you think of the dumbest things, she said to herself. Why, after having lived so much and put so many things behind her, had she concluded that the empty house was a symbol of uselessness? Then, with one single detail—the curtain hanging in the hallway, for example—the magic or whatever you call it stirs in you and makes you see the outlines of things, or makes you see what earlier had seemed so disastrous in a different way? Or could it be that those uncomfortable sensations of destruction and uselessness pertained to another time, to another occurrence, to another space? Could it be that as soon as she had entered her house, it suddenly appeared to her, that despite everything, it just had to screw things up, and since it was already in the apartment roaming around, to get inside her and beat on her? And to finish her off, even though everything seemed logical, cause and effect, Bernardo's outrageous idea of an underdeveloped Fred Astaire had interfered, combining with her notion of the Secret and Judicial Police. And although she couldn't differentiate between them, she knew perfectly well how they operated, their procedures, and that all of that together was nothing more than if, at first, you sense the destruction, then later, another symbol will appear complete with its entourage: the symbol of the buffoon, because the buffoon and his agents repress, destroy, make everybody's life and all things worthless. Then, wasn't it more significant that the idea of an underdeveloped Fred Astaire should appear and then, only then, the feeling that everything had been destroyed, and that if you didn't think along those very lines, something or someone was switching the order of the occurrences, of the sensations, of the persons? And where, then, should we place the revolution-words and the silence of the newspapers and Víctor Jara? Shouldn't we make a place for them, because even with all the light we've shed upon them weren't they placed in order according to a supposed dialectic, forming part of that same inverted order?

Couldn't it be that before entering her home that disorder was already in place, or perhaps she had picked it up on the street: a disorder felt even though it was not seen, or not conceived, but that had undeniably been caused by something or someone who customarily, on other days, at other times, didn't exist, but now disturbed that commonplace order-disorder where she functions, walks, eats, pays for things, defecates, greets others, and begins to walk again until she passes through the door of the building, climbs the stairs, opens the door of Apartment 402, and zap, there it is, that feeling that should have appeared in some other space, in another situation, at another time, maybe half an hour before, three hours after, four days, a week, two months? In some other house, another sofa, some other Georgina, some other Bernardo?

When Bernardo caressed her hair, Georgina was slightly startled.

"I didn't hear you coming."

"I didn't want to make noise because of Carla. You're going to burn yourself."

"What a dummy! I didn't realize. It's just that . . . "

"You really look tired."

"Why don't you go to bed? I want to read a while."

"Wouldn't you like to go a round with me? For a long time I've been thinking that maybe . . . "

Bernardo smiled, sat down next to Georgina, slipped his arm behind her shoulders, gave her a kiss on the neck.

"Wouldn't you feel better if you took a little nap?"

"Probably, but right now I've got the urge, can't we?"

"Let's do it."

"This is in our way."

Georgina quickly took off her blouse.

"And this too."

Now Bernardo started taking off her skirt. Georgina helped him by lifting her legs. Then Georgina removed her pantyhose. All she had on now were her brassiere and panties; she became flushed. She reached out to Bernardo and he reciprocated with pleasure; he quickly kissed her behind the ear and then drew away from her slightly to caress her breasts through the brassiere. For a brief, passionate moment he fondled them. Then his hands slipped to Georgina's back; finding the clasp, he pulled one of the straps upward and the other one downward so that the brassiere no longer imprisoned her. Georgina lifted her arms and Bernardo slowly removed her brassiere, as though he were disconnecting the detonator of a submersible mine. Now Georgina's breasts were free. Georgina raised her chest a little, offering them openly and determinedly, without reluctance, those same breasts that were now hardening at the tips, at the nipples, always small, but wondrous, exciting. Bernardo dropped his head between her breasts, turned his head to one side, and his mouth found and played with her small but wondrous nipples, his hands, meanwhile, were caressing Georgina's hips. Moments later, after he had nibbled on her breasts, after her hips and buttocks had been exhaustively entertained and his penis was firmly erect, the bodies found each other, overlapping, crossing: easily a leg could be mistaken for an arm and where a leg began and ended could not be determined. Georgina whispered in his ear, go ahead. Bernardo responded by unbuckling his belt, lowering pants and underwear at the same time with difficulty, while she lowered her panties hurriedly. Georgina was completely naked and Bernardo left his shirt on, but neither of them noticed the difference in their nakedness because Bernardo had already plunged into Georgina and she began to slowly move her hips. Georgina's desire was satisfied: now they were making love. They didn't hesitate, and their bodies were ready. Consciousness was no longer important—the hands, her breasts, his erect penis, the matted hair, her undulating vagina, these were the craftsmen of satisfaction. They weren't in a hurry because their lovemaking followed a syncopated rhythm. Georgina wrapped her legs around Bernardo as if other arms were resting upon Bernardo's hips. Let's turn over, Bernardo proposed. They tried to turn without separating, but since they did not succeed, they quickened the process and Georgina settled down on Bernardo, who already had her nipples between his fingers. While changing positions it seemed that urgency had taken over: the rhythm became more accelerated without becoming the agitated movement that at other times had brought them to pleasantly finalize what also had been gratifying earlier—syrup and mouth upon a nipple. Georgina straightened up a bit until she was completely seated, Bernardo looked up at the dance of her skin, Georgina smiled down at him, offering him through the slit of her eyes a passageway into her consciousness, as if saying, it's O.K., then, it's fine, this is wonderful, so, within one another, seated on you, sharing this refined syrup, yes, we're doing fine, let's keep going. Georgina just now realized that the tilt of her head, the slit of her eyes, coincided with the one formed by the union of the two large window curtains; then, through the slit of her eyes she noticed the cars passing on the street, and realized that there were people engaged in other things—walking, greeting each other, walking away—while she and Bernardo, engrossed in what they were doing, what they had decided to do after their chores, after their comings and goings. She stopped looking at the street and looked for Bernardo's face, looked at him with those same eyes which before had acknowledged the fine fit of their bodies while making love, based on the reference point of the comings and goings on the street. Her hips maintaining the rhythm of their movement, she smiled and turned her head to look again through the slit, searching again for the reaffirmation of their organs enjoying and sculpting themselves; and at that point, she now realized that on the sidewalk across the street, right in front of the store, were two parked cars; men got out, went around to the trunks, and took out what might be said to be weapons, Georgina felt a fierce, piercing shiver, as if they were already pounding on her stomach with their machine guns, she tried to separate from Bernardo, he held her tight, perhaps thinking that Georgina wanted to change her position, she remained where she was; all of a sudden she was no longer seated on Bernardo, the day was no longer crowned with glory, it was like today would not end until another day, probably not even tomorrow nor two months from now, she let Bernardo continue his movements and her tears, tears that understood a different dialectic, ran down that same face that just a while earlier had been caressed by small rings of smoke and, perhaps, because everything was so well prepared, and the pieces fit together perfectly, she thought that the feeling she had upon arriving home corresponded with this very moment.

a night for news

Bernardo had gone away for the weekend; thus for the time being the possibility of their killing him was postponed for at least a couple of days. But the danger of their coming after us won't disappear with a wave of the wand. They could detain me for questioning, just for questioning, as they say, even though my fingers aren't in the pie. Mom has no idea what could really happen, although she has suspected something ever since Bernardo was jailed in '68; Mom doesn't have an inkling that at any moment they could show up, while she warms my supper. She laid aside the half-finished vest she was knitting for Dad and her well-ironed bedspreads and even her hand-crocheted table covers. Dad is also acting like the world just stopped turning, because he's resting, thinking that everything happens out in the street just so Jacobo Zabludovsky can broadcast his timely news items, because Dad is right there, sitting in his easy chair, not worried about anything, watching and smoking one Del Prado cigarette after another.

Neither Mom nor Dad knows that just a little while ago when I went to put the car in the garage there was a blue minivan parked on the corner, just like the one that took Joel away; and they don't know that before I put the car away I went for a spin down to Camarones Circle just to throw them off my trail, and that on my way back a Dodge was already parked in front of the laundromat. Some of them were on one side of the street and others on the opposite side. So, they are either waiting for Bernardo to return home or it won't be long before they come up and "ask" about him, as if they were agents from the Monterrey Insurance Company.

Mom has brought me my meatballs and, as if the three of us had agreed to remain silent for some sad reason, she just smiles at me, hinting that the meatballs were delicious because Dad had liked them and that the tortillas were warming, as I could tell by the aroma coming from the kitchen. Then, I see her heavy body disappear into the kitchen, and without her knowing it she has left behind the image of a faded apron wandering around the dining room. When she worries, she worries about Bernardo and the pain in Dad's back—those are her two greatest worries. When it comes to me, she has only tender looks and encouraging smiles because I'm now half-finished with my degree; for her, that's a good and right thing to do, and, above all, it represents our future security. On the other hand, Bernardo is her biggest headache, and this concern about her strange, bearded son has been growing since the book dealer stocked his shelves with scandalous little books by Mao and others by Marx and Lenin. Then she feels obligated to explain to guests that they are books we had to order for school, although the visitors, mostly relatives, know that I study medicine, that Bernardo is no longer a student, and that he has spent time in jail. But despite those facts, Mom has to justify the presence of those books in her house. The visitors, eternal busybodies, end up scaring her to death with that business about kidnaping and political prisoners, and Mom doesn't have any recourse but to accept the fact that Bernardo is a pain in the neck, and that Beatriz has left home, and it was Bernardo who told her to get the hell out.

Dad doesn't say a thing. He resorts to what is called psychological warfare: he gets mad at Bernardo for the slightest thing, and stops talking to him for a week, grumbling from inside his bedroom so that Bernardo will know his father is not pleased that his eldest son has gotten into politics. But later, when Dad forgets about opposing his wayward son, it seems like they are both in agreement. I see a twinkle in Dad's eyes when Bernardo has his meetings in our room, and then he even tells me to sleep on the sofa until that lazy bum Bernardo finishes debating the issues.

In those situations, what Mom suggests is that older people should let younger people work out their problems, that they shouldn't give them bad advice. And the reason she says that is because some of the friends that Bernardo invites to the house are already behind the times. The one who comes around the most is old enough to be Dad's brother.

But for the time being they seem content. Dad is nodding in front of the TV, Mom, the busy little bee, is washing the dishes and brings me a cup of coffee and another smile. The tacit agreement keeps us from talking. I'm quite aware that it's all because Bernardo left for a weekend in Cuautla, Morelos, just because he needed to (Mom's version) and to clear his head (Dad's version). But I doubt that his vacation is taking place at all because, I don't know, I don't want to exaggerate, but these last few days the meetings have become increasingly frequent: Bernardo was coming in after midnight. Outside the house there's a van and a car waiting, and right now, while Dad sleeps soundly, Jacobo Zabludovsky announces the first day of the hunger strike at the Spicer company and Bernardo appears in the front line.

a letter from witold the pirate

for Alvaro Mutis

That night of sorrow, overwhelmed by ominous dreams and restless sounds swarming behind him, the man sat before his *secretaire*, raised the delicate bamboo blind, arranged paper and inkwell, reached for the quill, dipped it in the ink and began to write as if he were only taking dictation from one of the voices that addressed him from his oneiric fog:

My Dove: After long nights of bewilderment, I have finally been able to read the phrases that you never uttered; it was best that you never spoke them. Charitable was your discretion and painful was my reading. From my perspective, you know only too well, I have the word of the Knight of Chinese Wood and I will fulfill it as I deem prudent, one silence after another. My hermeticism will be identical to the fruits of the message that no one will find in this bottle: "Within my heart, which is a green apple carved in mahogany, several distinct and capricious compartments have been constructed; if you open the box with the tiny drawing of a bird, you will find a glass die which has inlaid on all its sides the number that symbolizes the love I feel for you. Take it, look at it, turn it around between your fingers, observe its rounded edges, the product of the meticulous labor of my friend the Chinese artisan who died, charred by the fire of a dragon that had gone mad. Turn the die over in the palm of your hand, hold it still, weigh it, close your fist and feel the warmth of the light of the fireflies. Now, delicately put it away in whatever position you desire; that's fine, since any of its faces will give us the answer. For now, that little box is closed and is secured by a fine gold chain and a strong jeweler's lock; your small luminous cube has remained dozing within. In the end it was better that there be but one black patch upon the pirate's face, rather than the total darkness of the seas, right?

Witold."

The man left the pen in the inkwell, stood up, and walked to the window with heavy steps. He looked out at the night; the murmuring waves of the hidden sea comforted him. A strange gray cloud enfolded Witold like a heavy cape; from within it, at intervals, wailing voices could be heard.

mystical serpents

In the profound darkness of silence the black and the white serpents appear. They twist and entwine continuously, in search of a passage within themselves or a way to fuse their powers to achieve the luminosity that might give reason to their incessant swaying. Since the beginning of time, they have found themselves in this circumstance—which is not to be found in the void—and it is even doubtful that there ever was a beginning, since everything suggests that they are the serpents of the eternal need to create all things that perish. In their constant intertwining, they form diverse symbols that have produced a silent and infinite language in which, only by chance, a few sign systems repeat themselves within the expanse of time: a mythology, nonexistent history, eyes that do not wish to look into the void, waters that dampen only in reflection and thought, mouths that make no utterances but that, from time immemorial, are anxious to sing a world of objects, animals, and Beings, a world that dissolves and reappears in a game of surprises and brief moments of tedium until it returns to profound darkness in a distant space in time. In a surge of carelessness, after a series of complex gyrations, there began to be woven a new message, never before articulated in that infinite language, until the serpents, without ceasing the swaying of their bodies, brought their fanged mouths together, and in the very center of their gaze appeared the idea of a man of reptilian essence. Within the arms of the human figure was created the idea of a guitar being played by a siren. When at last the first chords were sounded, and the cavernous voice shattered the cosmic silence, a distant point of light appeared, grew, expanded, and the first day appeared. The white and black serpents, becoming transparent, finally dissolving into the original blue sky. But they remain tenuously united in the most sensitive filaments of those fundamental beings who began to dedicate themselves to the task of inventing song, love, life, and dreams.

fire wedding

a match, dressed up like a bridegroom, leaves for the church. Upon arriving, he learns from his match relatives that the bride has run off in the company of another match dressed like a lover. The bridegroom strikes his head against misfortune and a small bonze* appears ablaze beneath the cigarette.

*Buddhist priest dressed in saffron robes

certain deaths

i

When the drunk dies we put away the cork. When the drunk dies we cure our own hangover. When the drunk dies we get the hiccups. When the drunk dies we toast his absence.

ii

When the one-handed man dies, orthopedists come to the wake and the lame cry. When a lame person dies the orthopedists show up again and one-eyed people cry. When a one-eyed man dies orthopedists aren't aware of it and pirates cry. When a pirate dies we, his friends, divvy up the booty and all the women who loved him cry.

iii

When a handsome man dies, ugly men pin purple carnations on their lapels.

iv

When a beautiful woman dies, the other women put on their make-up and draw a delicate black line along their lower eyelid.

fatal station

Traveling in the subway, in a partially-filled car, I find myself seated, wearing a formal gray suit. I'm reading a book of essays, and from time to time I look out at some of the platforms where we stop, in order to keep track of the different stations. I then take the opportunity to glance at the people who surround me and, on one of those occasions, among other legs, I discover a nicely shaped female pair, although nothing out of the ordinary. Nevertheless, in a manner of speaking, they are put together in such a special way that they distract me from my reading. It happens that the one nearest to me is tensed and somewhat in front of the other, standing straight and firm; white legs that stand out or stand down from the hem of her black dress, wearing gray high-heeled shoes with a strap securing them in the back. The first foot turns completely around, leaving the ruddy heel exposed, while on the other foot the strap has fallen down, leaving the heel totally naked. When this thought passed through my mind, I began to undress in my mind, until I felt a pleasing sensuality welling up in my stomach, then, migrating down to my genitals. I also realized at that instant that I was confronted with a fundamental fact concerning one of my fetishes, and I understood that a heel without a strap is a diminutive breast without a nipple that presents itself to us in an aura of complicity, a social act that's all-too-well understood; it's a hot little buttock that appears erotically in all innocence, through the rear of a pretty woman's high-heeled shoe. It constitutes a measured public invitation to vex our spirit without anyone being the wiser, not even the woman herself, whose face we have never seen. We arrive at the fatal station. The human geometry rearranges itself, and I fully regret having committed myself to attend a literary conference.

i love you

"Do you really love me?" the beautiful woman asked, rolling her gray eyes.

The adolescent looked at her intently, tenderly, nervously. With a slight tremble on his lips he searched within the dampness of his mouth for the perfect words.

"It's the first time I ever said I loved someone."

The woman smiled and turned her head to one side, making her beautiful short hair flutter momentarily. She looked at the young man who was coming to grips with his most intimate sentiments while leaning casually against a tree in the park at nightfall. She unbuttoned her long blouse and her lace brassiere, allowing her firm and smooth breasts to fall out. The man observed them tenderly, excitedly, fearfully. Overwhelmed by the excitement of the moment, the girl made a strange maneuver with her wrist, formed a crease in her skin, and thrust her hand inside her chest; she searched behind the horizontal lines of her thorax, pulled out her heart, and handed it to the boy.

"You're really going to give it to me?" he said.

"I love you too," she answered, without lowering her arm.

The young man took it, looked at it. From his leather bag he removed a white handkerchief to cover the heart and then he put it away. Meanwhile, she began to button her blouse, and her gray eyes were the fine mist of humid mornings, love letters made of sensual cigarette smoke, the mysterious fur of a gray cat peering out through somnolent eyes, the chiaroscuro of an impassioned spirit.

Enveloped in that vast feminine gaze, he embraced the girl, kissed her, ran his fingers through her hair that naturally fell back into place. He took her by the waist and they walked down the streets and avenues of the night, in harmony with the lighted and unlighted windows, with the lamp posts, and the sounds of the city that began to disappear.

In the entryway of her house they kissed each other for the last time. He noticed a certain paleness in his sweetheart's face suddenly illuminated by the random light of a passing car. Trying to open his bag, he exclaimed:

"I'll give it back to you, put it back . . . "

"It's nothing. Don't worry; it's better off with you," she explained. "After you leave, I'll go to bed and sleep soundly. I'm going to dream about the evenings that we will have to love one another, about your brown eyes, about the gray boats with which we navigate the waters of happiness, clouds, joy. Don't you see? Go on, go to bed. You love me and I love you. Everything's fine just as it is."

The beautiful woman disappeared gracefully behind a red wooden door and the boy was left with that image reverberating in his body, as if a beautiful and precise photograph had been engraved on his skin. He walked toward home, blazing a new path, so as to walk through the newly invented nocturnal city.

In the solitude of his room, wearing his old pajamas covered with blue horses, he opened the leather bag, took out the heart, and unwrapped it. He held it in his hands, and looked at it without knowing what to think. His hands felt the vivid voice of the heartbeats and he began a dialogue of tenderness and impassioned skin, of sensations never felt before. An emotion, somewhere between pain and burning, radiated from his body in all directions; he then understood that love was greater than his body and could be an ever-flowing fountain. At that moment, the young man loved himself: loved his somewhat tattered shoes looking up at him from the fringe of the bedspread that barely brushed the floor; loved his books and notebooks; adored the walls of his room, the banners and the photograph of his team. He loved his pajamas. The boy calmly cried and kissed the heart over and over.

He wiped his tears and blew his nose. He placed beneath his pillow that fundamental fragment, turned out the light, lay down, and slept. And he dreamt that he was walking beneath a gray sunset in which, upon passing through a thin wall of fog, he saw a woman approaching, calling to him. There, between the sheets of deep sleep, the bodies were lifted up, they were caressed, undressed, they were moved, they were rubbed, penetrated, they were turned over and over, flexed, sweated, they were separated, they lay down, and went to sleep, dreaming that they were surrounded by fog and loving and sleeping and dreaming that they were loving, that they were sleeping, that they were dreaming, that they were loving, that they were sleeping, ssshhh, ssshhh, ssshhh.

worms

a

The earthworm is a penis from head to foot. The earthworm is blind and happy. When it makes love it is even blinder. The earthworm dresses as an earthworm. It didn't chose to be an earthworm. At the very moment that it emerges from the black earth, all sweaty, with the twisting of its arabesque language, it explains its nervous thoughts about eroticism. The earthworm is not the whole truth, although it may seem to be. It goes around stark naked and is never ashamed.

b

The water worm is used as bait to catch armadillos and anteaters. Fishermen who operate this way look ridiculous wearing rubber boots while perched in a tree in northwest Yucatán.

c

A flying fish hung himself using an earthworm during the final hours of dawn. It is impossible, the same source states, to hang yourself with a glowworm, but there are fakirs* who swallow them and then spit flying fish.

d

The glowworm is the daughter of the sun and the godmother of the firefly. The glowworm is a pen pal of the eel; usually, the latter sends telegrams.

e

The non-flying fish hung himself using a sky worm.

f

As people grow old, they forget about worms. Worms are always on the lookout for children who cut them up into slices, like when their mothers fix sausage and eggs. Or else the children hold them up against the sky in order to read their sensual contortions, or they stuff them in another child's ear, and squash them when they get bored. This is why the more mature worms believe that it's good that when people grow older they forget about worms. Only the poet digs his spoon into the earth to fill flower pots.

* workers of wonders and marvels

the pill bug

The best defense for the pill bug is to turn itself into an inoffensive BB. The pill bug is a small, ancient invention that usually goes unnoticed. For example, when you discover it by overturning a rock in the garden and it scurries off, it becomes a minute locomotive moving like crazy with no pre-established track. It's an armored vehicle from the very first tiny world war. The pill bug is a single BB with feet.

The armor of a pill bug runs horizontally, as if ready for an attack. In a diminutive museum in the very heart of Nottingham Forest, on the banks of the Trent, there are several tiny helmets, breast plates and stomach shields that belonged to ancient armor, dissected pill bugs. Rocks and tiles lying on top of leaves, weeds, grass or damp earth are the traditional castles of concealed pill bugs. Under the perfect armor of the pill bug there is absolutely no one. Pill bugs don't worry at all about the modern world. They live serenely under the historic tile that keeps them isolated, in the dark, distant, primitive, promiscuous, hermit-like, honest, just, shielded.

red high-heeled shoes for a beautiful woman

for Magali Lara

They dyed the shoes apple red. Red shoes look good on the shoe rack, on the dresser, or abandoned at the foot of the bed. Feet are important in red shoes. Sometimes red shoes think. They put buckles all over red shoes. Red shoes know how to wait. Red shoes are sincere. Red shoes are the heart of feet. Red shoes look like a beautiful woman. Red shoes go well with a tight-fitting dress or with a full one. Red shoes go well without a dress. Red shoes are half Gypsy. Red shoes are the lips of sensuality. Red high-heeled shoes are the friends of black high-heeled shoes. Red shoes love naked feet. Red shoes are painted with love. Red shoes attract tiny minotaurs. Red shoes are a dream-come-true for feet. Red shoes always carry a ballerina.

black high-heeled shoes for the beautiful woman with the red high-heeled shoes

for Lucía Maya

The beautiful woman dresses her feet at night by wearing black high-heeled shoes. Black shoes are painted with the dark face of the moon. Black shoes are made of India ink. Black shoes are respectful. Black shoes are of the splotchy type. Sometimes black shoes cry. Black shoes have subtle circles under their eyes. Black shoes are made of shadows. Black shoes smile at daybreak. Black high-heeled shoes are friends of red high-heeled shoes. Black shoes make themselves up with that beauty spot you have next to your mouth. Black shoes listen to us. Black shoes are the shifty eyes of our legs. Black shoes are mysterious. Black shoes aren't black just because. Black shoes are melancholy. Black shoes have a touch of desperate love. Black shoes are the *yes* of a *no*. Black shoes love naked feet or feet with white socks with geometric designs. Black shoes are the foot's negligee. To black shoes they've added a touch of sensual darkness. On occasion, black shoes are the never-ending tunnel of darkness for men. Black shoes are tolerant of insomnia. Black shoes are accomplices of cats. Black shoes play under the bed with little gray unicorns. Black shoes always carry a lady who's a dreamer.

yellow high-heeled shoes

for Naty García

The beautiful woman wears a continuous dawn in her yellow high-heeled shoes. Yellow shoes are a frank smile. Yellow shoes look like mangos. Yellow shoes like light-weight, multi-colored balls. Yellow high-heeled shoes don't get along too well with black high-heeled shoes. Yellow shoes are dressed up like summer. Yellow shoes like to twirl in the air and land upright on a horse's croup. Yellow shoes are colored with butterfly wings. Yellow shoes are always partying. Yellow high-heeled shoes are for spirited cartoon characters like Lucy, Little Lulu or Little Orphan Annie. Yellow shoes can be worn from Sunday to Sunday. Yellow shoes prefer open air meetings. Yellow shoes go well with an acrobat's sandals. Yellow high-heeled shoes play Chinese checkers with red high-heeled shoes. Yellow shoes look nice in a cage; they lay eggs and fly away like canaries. Yellow shoes always say *yes*. Yellow shoes were dyed with the brightest of stars. Yellow shoes accompany the leap of a jaguar. Yellow shoes are the sun of all shoes. Yellow shoes go well with tight-fitting wool dresses, either lime green or violet. Yellow shoes are a bell with no sound, but as shoes they are the closest thing to a song. Yellow high-heeled shoes always carry a festive woman.

white high-heeled shoes

for Maricela Castillo

Fairies colored the white high-heeled shoes with kisses. There are white shoes made of white bond paper. They made white shoes out of a full moon. White shoes are shy. White high-heeled shoes have received the sacrament of baptism. White shoes are not made of cheese. White shoes look pale. White shoes seem to be made of plaster. White shoes are pure spirit. Some white shoes are messengers. White shoes are the opposite of the stride of a panther. White shoes are stained with chalk. It's difficult to pick out a pair of white high-heeled shoes. White high-heeled shoes play chess and dominoes with black high-heeled shoes. On occasion, white shoes are premeditatedly white. Old white shoes look like new. White high-heeled shoes become vexed at the acrobatics of yellow high-heeled shoes. There are white shoes who are somewhat hypocritical. White shoes are made of clouds. Upon white high-heeled shoes terrible or beautiful love stories are always written. White shoes murmur in a clear voice. White high-heeled shoes are the feet's golden dream. White shoes are to be taken off at any time. White shoes make perfect victims. Sooner or later, white shoes will be red, black or blue. White high-heeled shoes are for the beautiful woman who has an angel.

gray high-heeled shoes

Behind the mist you will find a beautiful woman wearing solemn gray high-heeled shoes. Gray shoes are one with the nightfall. Gray shoes bring rain. Gray shoes cannot be worn without a purse. Gray high-heeled shoes always solve the problem. Gray shoes go well with summer and all of winter. Gray shoes go well with either a dry green- or wine-colored jacket, and with skirts or coats of these same shades. At night, all gray high-heeled shoes are brown. Gray shoes are for rain. Gray shoes don't lose their color quality with black umbrellas. One could in no way affirm that gray high-heeled shoes are conformists. Gray shoes are for the beautiful woman who is having her picture taken in black and white. Gray shoes are the wisest of all shoes. Gray shoes are of another century. Gray shoes are similar to tears brimming in the eyes. Gray shoes are always silent on the shoe rack. Gray high-heeled shoes are content on legs that enjoy being crossed and bounced up and down. Gray shoes do not lose patience, but know they have the right to become angry. One can carry on long conversations with gray shoes. Gray high-heeled shoes maintain a discreet friendship with black high-heeled shoes. They do not tolerate white ones, are condescending toward red ones, and think that yellow ones are a joke. Yellow high-heeled shoes believe that gray high-heeled shoes are arrogant. Gray shoes keep walking even while dozing. Gray shoes are the fancy of all shoes. Gray shoes are a light rain at the foot of the bed. Gray high-heeled shoes are the chiaroscuro of the spirit. Gray shoes are for enclosed spaces. Gray shoes are the *yes* and the *no*. Gray shoes are stained with cigarette smoke. Gray shoes bring clear skies. Gray shoes are for the beautiful woman who makes herself up with discreet elegance. Gray shoes are definitive and tender. Gray shoes can keep a secret forever. Gray shoes like feet wearing light-colored socks. Gray shoes are the recollection of rain. Gray high-heeled shoes carry a serene woman.

on the shoe rack

- Green high-heeled shoes are made of pears.
- Pink shoes are strawberries. Pink shoes are prone to swooning.
- Brown shoes are for the office or for working breakfasts.
- Blue ones, only once in a while, and never near the sea.
- Canary-yellow shoes go well on women who like to ride giraffes or pumas.